TIDES

by Betsy Cornwell

HOUGHTON MIFFLIN HARCOURT

Boston • New York

www.hmhco.com

The text was set in Van Dijck MT.

Library of Congress has cataloged the hardcover edition as follows:
Cornwell, Betsy
Tides/by Betsy Cornwell.
p. cm.
Summary: After moving to the Isles of Shoals for a marine biology internship,
eighteen-year-old Noah learns of his grandmother's romance with a selkie woman,
falls for the selkie's daughter, and must work with her to rescue her siblings from his
mentor's cruel experiments.
[1. Selkies—Fiction. 2. Love—Fiction. 3. Internship programs—Fiction. 4. Isles of
Shoals (Me. and N.H.)—Fiction.] I. Title.
PZ7.C816457Ti 2013
[Fic] —dc23
2012022415

ISBN: 978-0-547-92772-5 hardcover
ISBN: 978-0-544-30296-9 paperback

Manufactured in the United States of America
DOC 10 9 8 7 6 5 4 3 2

4500467121

The cure for everything is salt water: sweat, tears, or the sea.

— Isak Dinesen

i carry your heart (i carry it in my heart)

— E. E. Cummings

for Corey

 CONTENTS

PROLOGUE   1

one • TALES   3

two • SHORELINE   12

three • SECRETS   15

four • SUMMER   22

five • DAUGHTER   28

six • RESCUE   38

seven • SHOALS   46

eight • SQUALL   56

nine • POD   66

ten • SEAL   74

eleven • HEART   81

twelve • CAUGHT   84

thirteen • WAVES   88

fourteen • STORY   93

fifteen • LEDGE   96

sixteen • ANCHOR   103

seventeen • RISING   113

eighteen • SOURCE   120

nineteen • LIGHT   134

twenty · RIPPLES   143

twenty-one · SUNSET   154

twenty-two · UNDERTOW   162

twenty-three · LINE   169

twenty-four · CUSP   176

twenty-five · LINK   180

twenty-six · GONE   190

twenty-seven · SEARCH   197

twenty-eight · SINKING   204

twenty-nine · SEEK   209

thirty · CHASE   215

thirty-one · SKIN   226

thirty-two · FOUND   233

thirty-three · TRUTH   237

thirty-four · VOICE   246

thirty-five · CHANGE   264

thirty-six · EBB   275

thirty-seven · HARBOR   280

thirty-eight · LAND AND SEA   286

PROLOGUE

THE color at the bottom is so deep, there are few who would call it blue.

There is light there — a little — for those who can find it. It shifts in the water, a vague, New England light. Just darkness unless you look carefully. If you want real light, you'll have to stay on the surface.

The Isles of Shoals have plenty of it, light that refracts off the salt-swept rocks and old whitewashed houses. Light that clinks its way over the waves like so much dropped and dented silverware.

It will hurt your eyes to look, on those bright summer days. You'll sit on the rocks until the spray dries and strings salt beads in your hair, but the brightness will eventually hurt.

Be careful. That not-blue of the deepest water will call to you, a seeming balm for your stinging eyes. But it will surprise you.

It's the shallow water you really want, what the Old Shoalers call the inbetween. It's that space between light and blue, land and sea, where the water is sometimes warm. The little fish swim there.

Once you're safe in the inbetween, you'll wonder why

you'd ever dare to broach the deep, with its hidden teeth and tentacles. You'll reject the white sun and dry salt above. For a while.

It's the colors that will make you stray. They sing to you, the not-blue and the searing light, and no matter how tightly you tie yourself to the inbetween, eventually you will break free.

No one swims only in the shallow water.

one

TALES

NO one is happy in the inbetween," said Gemm. "Not even selkies."

Wind moaned in at them through the windows. Gemm quieted, letting the weather have its interruption.

Her grandchildren stared at her, wide-eyed, mugs of tea growing cold in their hands. It didn't occur to Noah that he was far too old for these stories.

Well, that wasn't really true. The thought occurred to him — but in his father's voice instead of his own, as too many of his thoughts tended to do. *Gotta stop that.*

He glanced at his sister, Lo, seated next to him at Gemm's kitchen table. She was still wrapped in the story, her face open with wonder. She pushed aside a black length of hair that had fallen over her eyes. Noah wondered if she felt too old for fairy tales, too. These days, Lo seemed to think she was too old for everything.

Noah tapped the side of his mug. He hadn't come to the Isles of Shoals to listen to fairy tales. He had an internship at the Marine Science Research Center on nearby Apple-dore Island, and starting tomorrow he'd work long hours there until he left for college in August. If he did well, this internship would be his first real step toward becoming a marine biologist — something Noah had wanted since the first time his father took him fishing.

He remembered staring into the green water, watching a bluefish glint out of the murk and flash and fight as his father pulled it into the boat. The fish had been almost as big as five-year-old Noah, and he'd thought it was a monster, all metal-bright scales and spiked fins.

Noah loved that monster. He was desperate to know what else lurked and slept and waited in the water, and he knew he'd spend the rest of his life trying to find out.

That's why I'm out here in the middle of nowhere this summer, anyway, he thought. He was choosing this dream over every other consideration, something he'd done many times before — maybe too many times. Noah remembered all the nights he'd stayed up studying, all the dances he'd skipped, all the time he'd spent alone — so much that he didn't even mind, really, being alone. He kind of preferred it.

He'd worked so hard just to get here. Starting tomorrow, he'd work even harder. He told himself he'd earned the chance to feel childish once in a while, to listen to a fairy tale without overanalyzing everything. He tried to slip back into the rhythm of Gemm's story.

"The land calls to the selkies, sings to them, promises

of new knowledge and new joy. It whispers to them, and they cannot avoid its call." Gemm poured a thin stream of milk into her tea. Clouds bloomed in the dark liquid.

Noah closed his eyes and breathed in the ocean smell that filled his grandmother's cottage. The beating, shuddering wind outside led him deeper into the tale.

"They swim to the rocks and the beaches, and they shed their seal forms. They look like people, then. Humans."

The pale woman sitting beside Gemm — Maebh, she'd said her name was — took in a deep breath. The corner of her mouth twitched.

"Selkies need the land as we need the deep ocean," said Gemm. "They need it for its danger and its mystery. They come to the beaches and they sing. They sing to the ocean and the sky."

"Like sirens?" Lo asked. Noah knew she'd read the *Odyssey* in freshman English that year. He remembered reading it himself, but he preferred the part with Scylla and Charybdis, the two monsters on either side of your boat, with hardly any way to go between them.

"A bit like sirens," Gemm said, smiling. "Their songs are very beautiful. But unlike sirens, selkies don't mean you any harm with their songs. They don't sing to seduce or to kill. Their songs have nothing to do with anyone but themselves. They sing for the simple joy of it, and because of that, I imagine their songs are more beautiful than those of any siren."

Maebh and Lo both smiled at that.

Noah couldn't help staring at Maebh for a moment. It wasn't just that her skin was almost paler than white, as if she hadn't seen sunlight in years. He thought she must be about thirty, but something about her — the way she moved? — seemed much older.

Maebh's round dark eyes flicked toward his, and Noah lowered his gaze, embarrassed.

"In this story," Gemm said meaningfully, as if she knew Noah hadn't been paying attention, "there is a young fisherman, the handsomest in his village. Many women noticed him, wanted him — even loved him. But he never loved any of them back. Some said his true love drowned when they were children. Others said he was simply too proud, thought himself too special for any of the village women.

"He enjoyed his life, his fishing, but he wasn't satisfied. He often wandered the beaches at night, so handsome, but empty around the eyes. He brought a satchel with him to collect shells and sea glass and the like, but none of those things made him happy for long. He was looking for something — anything — that would satisfy him."

Maebh stiffened in her chair. Her large round hands twisted together in her lap.

Gemm continued her story, unaware. "Once, just on the cusp of autumn, the young fisherman wandered on the beach very late into the night, and he heard something. It was a sort of music that trickled through the air, low and sweet and eerie. He started to run, rushing over the rocky shoreline, careening around boulders and tide pools, hunting the source of that beautiful sound.

"He tripped and fell onto a patch of sand. Blood trickled down a gash in his cheek, and his hands stung with scrapes. But the pain in his body was already fading away, borne out to sea by the wonderful songs he heard. He had found the source of the music."

A slow, reluctant tear slipped down Maebh's cheek.

Now Noah's mother's voice came into his head. *Your grandmother's selfish, remember,* she'd whispered to him, just before she and his father had left the island that afternoon. *She's always lost in her own world, and she'll pay no attention to yours.* And then she had hugged him, just a little too tight, and walked out the door in her cloud of department store perfume.

Noah hadn't really believed her. After all, Gemm had agreed to let Lo and him live with her for the summer — she couldn't offer that much and be so very selfish. But now, seeing her rush on with a story that clearly upset her friend, Noah wondered. He watched Gemm while she spoke, willing her to look back at him.

"The music came from a group of people standing on the shore. They looked like no people the fisherman had ever seen — certainly no one from his village. A tall, elderly woman led the singing, and the others — there were perhaps two dozen — danced or waded in the surf or lounged on the rocks and sang to the moon that loomed above them, pale as their skin.

"It was one of these last that caught the fisherman's eye. She sat on a boulder in the shallows, a small distance away from her companions. She was folded in on herself, resting her chin on her hands, and her hands on her knees. She sang in a clear, true alto that vibrated with some matching sound, some answering call, inside the fisherman himself.

"He realized he had forgotten to stand back up after his fall. He pushed himself quietly to his feet, hoping the singers wouldn't notice him. But then he saw, down by his shoes, the thing that had tripped him. It wasn't a rock, as he had assumed, but something soft, yielding under his touch. It glimmered a little in the moonlight, like velvet — though the fisherman was too poor to have ever seen real velvet.

"Once he held it in his hands, he recognized it: a seal-skin, but larger and darker and finer than any the fisherman had seen before. He knew it must belong to a selkie. In that moment he knew who the singers were, and he knew what he must do."

Maebh covered her mouth, but they all heard her choked sob.

Gemm stood and took Maebh's hands in hers. She crouched down before her, so that their eyes were level. For a moment, they simply looked at each other. Then Gemm gently touched her hands to Maebh's cheeks and brought their foreheads together—a gesture so intimate, it made Noah look away.

His eyes settled on the photos that almost entirely covered the far wall. Their gold-painted frames glowed against the drab whitewash. A picture of Noah on the day he was born hung there, as well as the blurry photo of Lo that the Chinese orphanage had sent over a few months before her adoption. A formal portrait from their parents' wedding held a prominent spot, too. There were a few bigger frames around the edges that displayed yellowing pages cut from old magazines. They were clothing advertisements featuring a much younger Gemm. Noah had forgotten that she used to be a model.

Gemm looked beautiful in every one, but blank somehow, as if she'd been whitewashed too. There was something hollow in her brightest smiles. Noah thought about how she looked now: strong and weathered, present, happy. He preferred this Gemm, the Gemm he knew.

Noah turned back when he heard the squeak of Maebh's chair.

"I must leave now," she said in her faint, unplaceable accent. "It was wonderful to meet you, children. Goodbye."

Noah nodded at her politely and returned her goodbye. "It was nice to meet you, too," he said, even though he really thought she was a little strange to sit so quietly all evening and then cry at a fairy tale.

"Goodbye, Maebh," Lo said, rising from her chair. She shook the older woman's hand, and just for that moment, Noah thought she looked like a grown woman too.

Then Lo turned to Gemm and asked, "You are going to finish the story, aren't you?" Maebh winced a little, and the grown-up spell was broken. Lo was his bumbling little sister again.

Gemm glanced at her friend and smiled sadly. "It's getting late," she said. "I'll just show Maebh out."

Arm in arm, they walked outside.

A gust of wind rushed through the open door and whistled over Noah and Lo. They found a warmer spot on the old pink couch by the stairs.

"How can it still be cold in June?" Lo asked.

Noah laughed and tossed her the nubby blanket that hung over the couch's worn armrest. Their dad probably would have made a crack about Lo being insulated against the cold. She had been such a skinny baby, he'd say. Was New Hampshire really so much colder than China that she had to get fat just to keep warm?

Noah tried to push down the anger that rose in his chest whenever he thought about his father and Lo. It was one more reason he was glad he could take them both away from their parents for the summer.

Lo had a still, sad look on her face, and Noah guessed she was remembering their dad's "jokes" too.

He cleared his throat. "I'm hungry." His back popped as he stood and stretched. He heard the door open again.

"I've got just the remedy," Gemm said, pushing the door closed behind her. She didn't lock it — but then, thought Noah, why would she need to? Hers was the only house on the island.

She pulled a bag of chocolate chip cookies from the cupboard. Noah pretended he didn't see Lo close her eyes.

Gemm opened the bag, and a sweet pastry smell puffed into the air. "I ordered these special from the mainland," she said. "They're from my favorite bakery." She pulled a large, golden, chocolate-studded cookie out of the bag and offered it to Lo.

Lo sighed. She took the cookie and stuffed it in her mouth, already looking guilty.

"Not like that, sweetie," said Gemm. "These are special. Savor them." She took a small bite. "Delicious."

Lo's tears didn't quite come, but they shivered over her eyes like a rising tide. She wrapped the heavy wool blanket around her body and shuffled up the stairs.

Gemm opened her mouth to call after her, then closed it again. She looked at Noah, and he shook his head. Gemm raised her eyebrows but turned away, saying nothing.

Great, he thought. *This summer is off to a perfect start.*

two

SHORELINE

SUMMER was coming, and the islands were filling again.

Mara's shirttails spun in the wind, exposing, now and again, the strong muscles of her thighs. She tightened the knot on the length of frayed rope around her waist.

There were maybe fifty people on the lawn in front of the Oceanic Hotel, more than there had been this time last year, she was sure. For at least the tenth time since she'd arrived on Star Island that afternoon, Mara wished she could join them. But it was a stupid idea — what would she have to say? Besides, her family didn't like her to draw attention to herself.

She wrapped her arms around her waist to ward off the June breezes, still cold when they really got going. The Isles of Shoals were rocky and sparse, without even a grove of trees to soften the wind. She could see nearly all of Star Island and the eight other isles around it: the hotel, the fishermen's houses, the science center on Appledore, the lighthouse on White.

She pulled on the hem of the buttoned men's shirt she wore as a dress, wiggling her toes in her too-small sandals. She envied the tourist children their perfectly fitted clothes and shoes. Mara had only one outfit—she contemplated the word with amusement—that fit right, and it wasn't much use on land.

Smoke rose from a barbecue pit near the hotel kitchen. Curls of scent, bitter and fleshy and sweet, wafted over to her. She wished she could stay for dinner.

She scanned the groups of people that wandered over the island. The youngest children toddled between cooing guardians with outstretched arms, and their older siblings played soccer or lounged on the grass with stacks of summer reading. Teenagers milled around the edges of things, laughing and whispering to one another.

Mara took three steps toward them before she managed to stop herself. She knew the pleasure of a new friend wouldn't be worth the risk it involved. Tourists tended to find her a little too charming, a little too "local color." Her accent caused trouble, too. Better just to stay out of it.

The salt was dry on her skin now, and the sky was almost dark. Mara told herself it was time to go. She wanted a swim before she went home, and her brother would be cross if she didn't return soon to help him with the younglings.

She crept to Miss Underhill's Chair, the rocky outcropping on the northeast side of Star. She watched a fishing boat come around the side of the island, trailing a large net.

As it crossed in front of her, the man at the wheel met her eyes. She waited for him to pass.

Once she made sure she was alone, she climbed down the steep rocks, into the shadows.

She tucked her shirt, sandals, and belt into the crevice she found there, the one she always used. She wished she had something better to wear, but there hadn't been much left behind at the end of last summer, and Mara hated to steal outright. She'd just have to hope someone would leave behind a pair of shorts or a sundress when the hotel closed in the autumn.

Autumn. Mara wrinkled her nose. The islands were safer when summer ended, when most people were gone, but they were boring.

She sat on a rock and shrugged her body down into the water. It felt light and sweet against her skin, like kisses, or what she thought kisses must feel like. There wasn't much opportunity for kissing when she couldn't talk to people outside her family.

Mara slipped the rest of the way under, letting the cold water stop her thoughts.

She pushed off from the rocks and swam away.

three

 # SECRETS

Lo woke up early.

Her phone whined at her from the dresser across the room, where she'd put it so she couldn't just turn it off and keep sleeping. She sighed into her pillow.

She heard Noah groan from behind the folding screen that divided the guest room. Guilt got her up then—she didn't want to wake him up at this ungodly hour just because she had work to do. Let him sleep a little longer.

She pulled herself out of bed, shuffled over to her dresser, and picked up the phone. It took a few moments to find the right button, her eyes still bleary with sleep. When the electric bleating finally stopped, the silence filled the room.

Then Noah let out a great rattling snore. Lo smiled. She didn't need to worry about waking him up—he'd once slept through the smoke detector alarm when they were kids.

Lo pulled a shirt out of the second drawer and laid it, still folded, on her bed. She repeated the process with

15

every other item of clothing she needed until she had a neat pile of fabric stacked on the blankets, a Cubist version of her outfit for the day. She closed her eyes when she put on her clothes, tugging them up her legs or over her head and trying not to think about it. She could feel the rough edge against her neck where she'd cut the size tag off her shirt. She wiggled her shoulders to get rid of the itch, but it didn't help.

Lo really meant to walk downstairs right then, but there was a mirror hanging on the door, and her reflection caught her as she tried to leave. She saw a glimpse of double chin and round cheeks before she tore herself away. She started to slam the door shut, then remembered her still-sleeping brother and grandmother. She could hear the mirror laughing at her as she gently closed the door.

The sunrise glow coming in downstairs made her feel a little better. She looked out the north window, and her breath caught.

From here the isles seemed set in a circle, like a crown. The air was so clear that everything—the buildings, the grass, the rocks—looked closer and farther away at the same time. The rising sun turned it all golden or shadow blue. Only the water was solid, impenetrable, and it sparkled like metal under the sky.

Lo opened the window, and the kitchen breathed in air and light. She smiled.

She thought about eating breakfast, then told herself she wasn't that hungry. She put a kettle on the stove for tea instead.

Her real reason for waking up early waited for her by the door. She dug through her backpack, the one bag she hadn't bothered to bring upstairs when they'd arrived yesterday. Two of Noah's bags still lay slumped against the wall, half open, his socks and shirts spilling out. She sighed and poked his clothes back into place.

She took out her sketchbook and a few thick sheets of watercolor paper, stacking them neatly on the table. Her pencil set came next, and a small box of paints.

Lo's fingers lingered over the different pencils, and she chose one of the lightest for her first sketches. She looked around the kitchen, searching for a good subject.

The kettle whistled. She got up to take it off the heat —and Maebh appeared at the top of the stairs, coming out of Gemm's bedroom.

Lo jumped, and the empty mug in her hands clattered to the floor.

Maebh stepped back, and a worried line deepened between her eyebrows. With one hand, she pulled her green bathrobe tighter around her chest. Lo knew that robe— her mother had sent it to Gemm for Christmas a few years ago. Maebh's other hand stayed behind her back.

Silence flooded the room.

Maebh cleared her throat. "You're up early, dear."

Lo looked down. "You, too." She wasn't sure what else to say. Inside, she was remembering things, working things out.

Ever since she could remember, her mother had called Gemm unfeeling, irresponsible, and selfish. Lo figured out a long time ago that that was mostly because Gemm and Gramps got divorced when Mom was in college, and Mom had sided with Gramps. Lo still didn't know the reasons behind the divorce, and she'd never felt a pressing need to find out.

But now Maebh stood in front of her, wrapped in Gemm's bathrobe, on the threshold of Gemm's bedroom. The casual expression Lo was trying to maintain slipped off.

She grinned at Maebh as if the woman were a winning lottery ticket. Finally, she understood. Lo tried to wipe the smile off her face. She couldn't.

Maebh still trembled in the doorway. Lo thought she saw a chagrined sparkle in her eyes, but it quickly faded.

"Well." Maebh let out a long breath. "You look to have figured everything out right quickly, Lo." She tilted her head to one side, a look of pleading on her face. "Dolores was hoping to tell you. She didn't want to keep secrets. She just thought she would test the waters first, if you will."

Lo knew Maebh was trying to ask her for something, but she didn't know what. Her blessing? Forgiveness? She thought for a moment before speaking again. "I thought she must be very lonely, out here by herself. I'm glad she has you." She offered Maebh a gentle smile and received one in return.

"She is a bit lonely sometimes. I have a family to look after, myself."

Lo remembered how silently Maebh had appeared. She realized she had been trying to slip out. "Please don't let me keep you," she said. Fascinating as this had been, Lo was eager to open her sketchbook and get back to work. It was easier to ignore her hunger when she was drawing.

Maebh walked down the stairs. She paused for a moment at the bottom of the steps, then crossed the rest of the space between them. Lo noticed for the first time how small Maebh was. The top of her head barely came up to Lo's ears.

"She loves you very much, you know," said Maebh. "She's missed you both." She put a light, soft hand on Lo's cheek. For a moment, under Maebh's gaze, Lo felt as if she could do no wrong. It was a strange feeling.

Maebh nodded, as if Lo had passed some test. She turned, silent — still wearing Gemm's robe — and walked out the door.

Strange, Lo thought, to wear a bathrobe outside — but maybe Maebh was going swimming. Anyway, it certainly wasn't the strangest thing about that morning. She sat once more and opened her sketchbook — and realized the tea-kettle was still whistling. She got up and was just filling an infuser with Earl Grey when she heard another creak on the stairs.

It was Noah, still in his pajamas, his sandy hair sticking out in every direction. He hated mornings even more than Lo did. She doubted he even noticed her standing there as he slunk toward the cottage's one bathroom, towel and shampoo in hand.

Lo heard the click and swish of the shower turning on. The white noise wanted to lull her back to sleep, but she returned to the table and picked up her pencil again.

She was still looking for the right thing to draw when Noah reappeared. He was fully dressed now, with his unruly hair tamed, at least for the time being. He had always been tall and lanky, his arms and legs too long for his frame, but it was starting to suit him. Lo was glad her friends wouldn't see him this summer. They tended to moon over him a little too much.

In his MARINE SCIENCE RESEARCH CENTER STAFF shirt and new khakis, Noah really did look like a scientist. He kept putting his hands in his pockets, taking them out, and putting them back in again. He looked at Lo; he looked out the window; he looked at the door. He exhaled.

Lo groaned. "Hey, big brother," she said, "you'll do great."

Noah looked startled for a second, then smiled back at her. He could never manage to smile evenly — the right side of his face always dimpled. It was the only thing that could make him look mischievous.

Lo walked over to him, stood on her tiptoes, and scruffed up his hair. "There," she said. "You're good to go."

Noah nodded grimly, a slightly geeky soldier off to battle. He grabbed an apple from a bowl on the kitchen table, and with a last, panicked glance at his watch, he ran out the door.

Lo considered the two very different encounters she'd already had that morning. She shook her head. This was not starting out to be the private day of sketching she'd imagined.

She sat down and once again cast around for a subject. There were three apples left in the large wooden bowl on the table. They were all at least a little bruised, with dry leaves still attached to their stems. Lo thought about plucking off the leaves but decided they mostly looked fine the way they were. She turned the biggest one around to hide its bruises.

She put pencil to paper, letting her mind wander as her eyes and hands focused in on her drawing. She thought of Maebh, framed in the doorway to her grandmother's room. She wanted to tell Noah about it, but she'd talk to Gemm first. Lo held her new secret close, tucked deep in a locked chest of secrets inside her.

four

 SUMMER

NOAH rushed through the hall to catch Professor Foster before he disappeared into his office again.

"Professor—" he called. "Professor Foster, wait!"

The older man turned around, a smile placed carefully among the tired lines of his face.

"Hello there, Mr. Gallagher." He sighed, not quite letting the smile slip. "What can I do for you?"

"I, well . . ." He'd been so sure Professor Foster would want to talk to him, but it was obvious all he wanted was to be left alone in his office. Noah hadn't quite thought that being an intern would feel so . . . insignificant. He'd beat out dozens of other kids—college students, even—for this job, and he'd thought it meant he was special, or at least that Professor Foster thought he was. He couldn't quite believe filing checks and tax exemptions was really all he was meant for this summer.

Blood flamed over his cheeks and forehead. "I just wanted to know if there was anything else I could help you with, sir." He glanced back as a trio of researchers moved

~ 22 ~

through the hallway, murmuring seriously to one another. His stomach ached with jealousy. "Or if there was anyone else I could help."

Professor Foster raised his hand to his temple for a moment, an overloaded key chain hanging from his thumb. "I've got you where you're most needed right now, Mr. Gallagher. I'm sorry." Another fraction of his tired smile vanished.

"Oh." *Don't sulk*, he told himself. *It won't help anything.* "Well, let me know if you need anything else. I'm just—I just want you to know I'm really excited to be here."

Professor Foster sighed. "I know. We're excited to have you. Just—" He glanced back into his office. "Just keep at it in the filing room for now, and maybe I'll find something else for you later in the season." He looked back toward Noah, his blue eyes glinting through his wire-rimmed glasses. "You seem like a smart kid, Mr. Gallagher. Just show me you can do what I need you to do, and well . . . then we'll see what else I can find for you." He nodded, and his smile ticked for a moment into something more genuine. "You see what I'm saying?"

"Yes, sir." Noah smiled back and almost meant it.

Professor Foster closed his office door behind him, and Noah walked back into the main lab. He wound his way through it, trying not to stop and stare at every single project going on around him. He turned down a small hallway lit with overly bright but flickering fluorescent bulbs and walked all the way to the door at its end. He turned the doorknob, but he had to push his shoulder against the humidity-swollen plywood before the filing room opened for him.

It was dark and it was dank and it smelled like old paper. It smelled like his father's office, like the guidance counselor's room at his high school, like every cramped indoor place in the world. The light was flat and dismal, the carpet brown. There was a window on the far side of the narrow room, but it was covered by stacks of boxes, and it would be for at least another few weeks.

Noah decided that would be his first goal. He'd get through enough boxes to clear the window, and then maybe, just possibly, he could actually see the ocean.

That was why he'd come here, really. That was all he wanted. To see the ocean, every day. Every minute.

To learn from Professor Foster too, if he could get half a chance. He'd managed to audit the professor's Intro to Marine Science course at UNH last fall. It was one of the most popular classes on campus, and it filled up quickly every semester, so he'd had to beg for his registration, just for permission to sit in the back of the crowded lecture hall and listen, and in the end his biology teacher had had to call in a favor to Professor Foster himself.

And just like every college freshman in the room on the first day of class, he'd seen in an instant how brilliant Professor Foster was. The man glowed with energy and love for his subject with every word he spoke. He'd had tenure at UNH for quite a while, but he acted and looked like a much younger man than he was. His obvious passion had hooked into something inside Noah, something that had been there since the first time his father took him fishing. That something spread tingling all through Noah's body, and he knew, he was completely sure, that all he wanted out of college was to go to UNH and study marine science and be Professor Foster's student.

And thanks to that same high school biology teacher, he'd gotten a glowing recommendation that had landed him an interview for this internship even though all the other applicants were college students already.

Noah had walked into the interview with sweaty palms and a tie that felt too tight around his neck, especially when he swallowed. Professor Foster's office door — his office at UNH — was closed, and he'd had to knock.

"Come in," the professor had called, his voice a touch deeper and slower than Noah remembered from class.

Noah had stepped carefully through the door, his back as straight as he could make it. He'd looked Professor Foster in the eye the way his dad had told him to.

"Hi, Professor Foster. I'm Noah Gallagher. I'm here for the interview. I know you probably don't recognize me, but—"

"Back of the classroom." Professor Foster nodded. "Taking notes like a madman. More than most of the actual students. I certainly remember." He extended a callused, strong-looking hand. "Gary Foster."

Noah took his hand and shook it, hoping his grip was right. "Noah. Gallagher." He grinned, he hoped not too foolishly. "I'm really excited I might get to work with you this summer, sir."

He'd sat down as Professor Foster settled back in his desk chair.

"So, Mr. Gallagher, what's your interest in marine science?"

And Noah had found himself spilling over with stories: the first time he'd gone fishing with his father, the other classes he'd practically abandoned for more hours in the science labs, the academic articles he'd started reading in his freshman year of high school, all the weekends he'd spent studying alone in his parents' house or the UNH library, or out on the beach or on the water—alone then, too. Alone except for the thing he loved.

Eventually he'd felt a dry catch in the back of his mouth and stopped to clear his throat. A slow-rising blush had crept up his face as he thought about the rant he'd just delivered.

Professor Foster stood and extended his hand again.

Noah took it, thanked Professor Foster for the interview, and walked away, convinced he'd utterly failed. But a week later, his biology teacher had greeted him with a "Congratulations!" and a beaming smile.

"You'll start in June, as soon as school's out," he'd said, shifting from foot to foot in squirming excitement.

For a moment, Noah had wanted to ask where, but of course he knew — he'd known right away.

He'd spent the latter half of his senior year paying even less attention to his other classes than before. After he'd gotten into UNH — on a cross-country scholarship — he'd done nothing but run and get ready for this internship. He knew it was supposed to go to a college student, and he wanted to be more than prepared.

And now he was stuck in a tiny, airless backroom, filing. For the whole summer. He might as well have stayed on the mainland and worked in his dad's office as his parents had wanted.

Noah let himself kick one of the crumbling boxes. Just one. Hard.

Then he sat down and got to work.

five

DAUGHTER

LO sat on the crest of White Island, squinting at the waves, sketchpad in hand. She wanted to try to draw the inbetween, the not-quite ocean not-quite land, the thing that soaked through her memory of Gemm's story.

She saw darkness under the water, and she saw the solid white glint of light on its surface. As hard as she tried, though, she couldn't see into the space between the two —at least not enough to draw it.

She flipped back to the sketches she'd made the night before. Seals and women swam in a fluid border around the edges of the page between swirling lines of India-ink water. Lo usually liked to start her new projects with pencil, but the dry, gray graphite hadn't seemed right for drawing selkies. A thin brush and a pot of blackest black ink had given her drawings the liquid quality she wanted, but there was still a blank expanse in the middle of the page.

Lo took a pen from the messenger bag at her side and twirled it between her fingers. She started drawing almost without thinking, more wet black lines for long hair, smooth cheeks, large eyes. She had a face somewhere in her mind, but she didn't recognize it until she leaned back to look at her finished work.

Long hair straight and black as her own. A round, pale mouth and soft cheeks. Black eyes huge and wide-set and sad, somehow older than the face that framed them. Maebh.

Lo smiled at the page, proud of the likeness she'd accidentally captured. Maebh was lovely — not with Gemm's bright and glowing kind of beauty, but muted, like sea glass. Lo rarely liked her drawings so soon after she'd made them, but she could see she'd brought Maebh's soft beauty to the page. She blew lightly on the paper to make sure the ink was dry, then carefully closed her notebook.

She looked up and realized she wouldn't have been able to draw a landscape just now, anyway. The light had changed too quickly. The clouds were clumping together overhead, and a cold shadow was seeping over the island.

She shivered. When she stood, her legs started to prick and tremble. She hadn't noticed them falling asleep.

Lo walked into the cottage and shut the door behind her. Gemm was reclining on the couch and reading a worn paperback copy of A. S. Byatt's *Possession*, another mug of dark tea steaming beside her. She put her book down when she saw Lo.

"A wonderful book — sad, though. But sometimes the sadness makes a story better, don't you think?" She smiled.

Lo made a vague agreeing noise. "Gemm," she said

tentatively, "do you think you could finish the selkie story now?" Lo didn't understand why her mind had hooked onto the idea of selkies so tightly. All she knew was that she really wanted to hear the ending.

"If you like," said Gemm. "That one has sad parts too, you know."

Lo shrugged. She sat down next to her grandmother, ignoring the heavy sound of the couch springs as she settled in, the sight of her thighs squashed against the cushion, the puff of fat where her legs met her shorts. *By next month*, she thought, *these clothes will be too big. By two weeks from now. Easy.*

"It's not even lunchtime," Gemm said. "I figured you'd still be asleep."

"I got up early." Lo looked down at the floor. "I saw Maebh before she left."

It was quiet.

Gemm started to get up, then sat down again.

Lo waited.

"Lo, there are lots of things you don't know about me. Things your parents don't necessarily approve of." She laughed, short and bitter. "Actually, there's just the one thing."

Lo looked up and saw that Gemm's mouth was set hard and that her fingers trembled in her lap. She placed a hand over her grandmother's.

"I love your mother," whispered Gemm, so quietly that

Lo had to lean forward to hear her. "But I couldn't live my whole life lying. I had to be the — the person I am."

Lo stayed quiet, sensing that maybe she didn't need to say anything at all.

Gemm met her eyes at last, and her face was open and sad. "The story," she said. "That might help. Now, where were we?"

Lo smiled. She'd been telling herself the beginning all morning. "He'd just found the selkie skin." She lowered her voice to imitate her grandmother. "He knew what he must do . . ."

Gemm took over without missing a beat. "The fisherman crouched there, hidden behind the line of boulders, and he watched the selkies sing." The sadness in her voice was gone now, as if she'd forgotten she was Gemm at all and had become only a storyteller. "Well, that young woman, who sat apart from the others, she was the most beautiful thing the fisherman had ever seen in all his life."

Lo smiled at that, though Gemm's voice stiffened when she said "thing."

"The fisherman ran his hands over the skin. He couldn't believe his luck. He folded it and tucked it carefully into his satchel. He wrapped it in a net to protect it from his gutting knife and the sharp edges of his shells.

"He closed the sack, blood thrumming fast through his veins. He turned around and saw shining black eyes looking into his. The selkie had come to him.

"She said nothing, but reached out and touched his cheek with her hand. He had claimed her sealskin, you see, and in doing so had placed her under his power. He brought his own hand up and clasped hers. 'Hello,' he said. 'You are beautiful.'

"The selkie said nothing. Her eyes were soft and metallic. 'You are the most beautiful thing I have ever seen,' said the fisherman then. Still nothing.

"He had heard the stories, but even now, with a selkie in front of him, he couldn't quite believe. He found he was afraid. But if taking her skin really kept her in his thrall as he'd heard it did, he would find out soon enough. He pulled her toward him. 'Come,' he said. He turned away, hoping, hoping, and took his first step.

"The selkie followed. Her family, her pod — they never saw her leave. The selkie followed the fisherman inland, her hand in his. They were married within the week."

Gemm shifted in her seat. The creak of the springs brought Lo back from the story's world. She heard waves beat against the shore outside. Light cascaded through the windows in pale banners. Lo was sure the story wasn't over, but Gemm stayed silent.

"Tell the ending."

Gemm turned her gaze away from the brightest window. "Sorry, honey?"

"Tell the end, please," she said. "What happened to the selkie girl?"

"Oh," said Gemm. "Happily ever after. The end."

"Tell it right!" Lo knew she sounded childish, but she couldn't help it.

Gemm smirked. "Well, she never spoke a word, though the fisherman often asked her to sing again. She never even said her own name. In the village she was simply 'the fish-wife.' Through her silence, the sound of her own name, sung by her kin, always echoed in her mind. She missed her home and her family, but she could never tear herself away from the fisherman, because he had her skin. She searched for it for years, but the fisherman had hidden it well.

"In time, the selkie and the fisherman had a child— a girl. She loved her daughter, even though the very sight of her reminded the selkie of her captivity. After she gave birth, she stopped looking for her skin. She tried to forget, for her daughter's sake. But she couldn't ignore her true self." Gemm's voice had strengthened, and the wrinkles in her forehead were deep and tight.

"One day, the selkie was sitting on the beach outside the fisherman's house, staring at the waves, weaving a net. The selkie made the best nets for miles around, and they brought in more trade than her husband's fishing ever did. She heard her daughter's footsteps behind her.

"'Mother,' said the girl, 'I found an old leather coat in the rafters. May I have it?'

"The selkie turned and faced her nearly grown daughter. She felt herself turning cold, and then warm.

"The selkie dropped her net and let it tangle in the surf. She ran into the house. There it was—there it was! She saw it almost as soon as she got inside. It was half pulled down from the rafters, where it had been hidden all those too-many years. It was dusty, dry, and cracked along the places where it had been folded. But it called to her.

"She reached out, struggling to believe. As she grasped it, her voice swam back into her body, tearing into her throat like a riptide. She coughed, and a mist of blood spattered over her lips. She clutched her lost skin, and on the sandy floor of her husband's cottage, the selkie wept. She cried and screamed until she was exhausted.

"When she finally looked up, her daughter was standing in the doorway. She was crying too, but silently.

"The selkie felt at once that her own voice had returned at the expense of her daughter's. She walked over to her child and embraced her. Already the sea rushed loud in her ears, pulling at her bones. 'I have to leave you now,' said the selkie—the first words she'd ever spoken to her daughter. 'I love you, but I have to go. You have grown up strong and good. You don't need your mother anymore.'

Her daughter's eyes clouded.

"'Would you come to the sea, then?' the selkie asked. 'You are my daughter. You could wear my skin. Would you come?' But her daughter said nothing, and the selkie knew she would not.

"She took up her skin and left the fisherman's cottage. She could not bear to look back. The beach was just ahead, the waves sweeping in and pulling back in a heartbeat rhythm. She shed her dress and waded in, then dipped her sealskin in the cold water and watched it come alive. She wrapped it around herself. Her seal and human parts melded together, and the selkie swam out to sea. She was herself once more.

"Her daughter had many suitors, mostly fishermen charmed by her silvery skin and the black depths of her eyes. Eventually she chose a husband. The selkie risked returning to human form for the first time since her escape to attend her daughter's wedding.

"But she was not welcome. The fisherman, you see, had hanged himself shortly after the selkie left. Her daughter would not listen, would not hear her protests that she had been kidnapped, that she had every right to escape.

"The selkie left the wedding party in misery. She wished she'd been forced to stay and dance in red-hot iron shoes, like bad mothers in other stories. She wrapped her graying sealskin around her shoulders and made her last journey to the sea. She was never seen on land again."

Everything was still. No steam rose from Gemm's mug. No wind battered the walls of the cottage. This time, Lo knew without asking that the story was over.

She looked around the room, reminding herself where

she was. She had watched the selkie slink away into the darkness—or she had been the selkie, and was only now coming back to herself. Gemm's house was cast in shades of gray. The wood looked faintly damp, the whitewashed walls powdery and thin.

Lo laughed softly—she couldn't think of anything better to do. Gemm offered a small smile, and Lo immediately felt guilty.

"I knew it wouldn't have a happily-ever-after," she said.

Now Gemm laughed. "Well, there will be a happy ending for us. It's lunchtime." She walked over to the refrigerator.

They made corned beef sandwiches. Lo ate two and excused herself. The bathroom was just off the kitchen, so she knew she had to be quiet. She waited until she heard Gemm fiddling with the dishes. Then it was just a matter of two fingers down her throat.

A hot, thick wave rose up inside her. She bent over the toilet and choked everything out. She had to fight for breath when she was done.

Lo stared at her face in the bathroom mirror. A blood vessel had ruptured on her cheek, and it spread like a road map under her right eye. She took concealer from her toiletry bag on the sink and dabbed at her face until it looked even again. She squinted at her reflection and scowled, then stopped. Her cheeks stuck out when she scowled.

When she had gargled and wiped her mouth, she left the bathroom. Maebh was in the kitchen now, eating a sandwich and talking quietly with Gemm. Lo couldn't quite hear what they were saying, but Maebh made shapes in the air with her large hands and Gemm leaned forward, listening intently. Her gray hair had escaped from its knot and hung down her back in pale streams. Maebh's hair was in braids again, curled into intricate patterns at the nape of her neck.

Maebh noticed Lo watching them, and she smiled at her. "Come join us, Lo," she said warmly.

Lo blushed, certain she wasn't wanted. But both Gemm and Maebh looked at her with nothing but kindness and interest in their faces. Lo nodded and took her seat at the table.

six

RESCUE

RUNNING usually kept Noah from thinking too much, but it wasn't helping yet. He kept thinking of the day he'd had and mourning the internship that could have been.

He remembered the visions he'd conjured up when he'd applied for this job: electron microscopes, bubbling test tubes, shark-tagging expeditions. He'd known, in a small and unacknowledged corner of his mind, that the real thing might not be that exciting. Still, he couldn't hold back the sinking disappointment he'd felt after arriving at the Center that morning.

Professor Foster had played a starring role in Noah's internship daydreams. Noah had heard the professor's voice in his head many times, saying how talented he was, the best student of marine science he'd seen in years. Professor Foster would eat lunch with him, discuss his latest research, and invite Noah into his advanced seminar at UNH.

For someone with low self-esteem, Noah thought to himself, *you really know how to build yourself up. Idiot.*

Noah knew making a good impression on Professor

Foster would open all the doors he needed—this summer, at college, and afterward. But he had obviously failed to show he could really be useful, and now he was stuck in the filing room for the rest of the summer. Professor Foster had claimed it was important work, but Noah knew better.

"We haven't gotten a decent grant in years," Foster had said, "so we still run a lot on donations. We've got about four decades' worth of request forms, replies, and receipts back here, and we need them all filed, first by name and then by date. You can enter everything into our server as you sort, and in the end we'll have this nice, shiny new database so we can figure out who's worth the price of the stamp we use to ask them for money."

Noah had nodded and smiled. He'd thought it wouldn't be so bad. But he'd barely gotten through one box of ancient, crumbling papers by lunchtime. He'd tried to keep himself from counting the remaining boxes, but he already knew how many it took to reach the ceiling, and about how big the room was, and his brain did the calculations before he could stop it. There were two hundred boxes—at least.

At the end of the day, he'd sorted through two and a half of them. Noah knew he would be lucky just to finish them all by the end of the summer. He filed away his dream internship with every wrinkly scrap of paper noting that some old woman had donated five dollars to the Center thirty years ago.

The filing room was dry and blasted with so much air

conditioning that Noah's ears were ringing and he still had goose bumps when he finally left at the end of the day. He thanked a distracted Professor Foster for the opportunity (for the umpteenth time) and walked out into the yellow island sunshine. He didn't want to do anything but run.

Noah knew it was his 5K time, not his brain, that had gotten him the scholarship he needed, much as he liked to pretend otherwise. His science grades were almost perfect, but in every other subject he struggled for his Cs and Bs. He wasn't going to let his dream get away from him by not being in shape when cross-country season came. He'd changed in the Center's bathroom, and at first he thought he'd just run on Appledore.

But staying on Appledore made him think too much. He needed to go somewhere else—not White, where Gemm and Lo would be waiting to pounce on him with questions about his first day. He settled on Star, the second-largest island, where at least he wouldn't have to pass the Center with every lap. Noah already liked Star Island best, anyway, he thought—it was very green, whereas Appledore was rough and sparse except where the Thaxter garden had been pushed into the unwilling earth. Star was probably green only because of some unrelenting fertilization by the Oceanic Hotel gardeners, but they still managed to make it look natural.

It took him five minutes to navigate the *Gull*, Gemm's

ancient red rowboat, from Appledore to Star. Gemm had an old motorboat, too: the *Minke*, named for the species of small whales that populated the ocean here. She'd laughed at Noah when he'd said he would take the *Gull*, but he'd told her he liked the idea of getting himself places on his own strength. She'd accepted that easily enough, and Noah had enjoyed rowing to work, though he wasn't very fast yet.

Noah tied off the rowboat at the hotel's pier. He stretched for a few minutes and then put his headphones back on, scrolling through his music until he found his running playlist.

He set off around the hotel, taking in deep, steady breaths. The carefully trimmed lawn bent under his shoes and gave off sweet fresh-mown smells. The wind kept him cool.

Noah approached a large memorial stone, a rough granite obelisk that was almost completely covered in gull droppings. Another statue stood next to it, small and squat and even dirtier. He saw dozens of tiny monuments around them, stacks of rocks and twigs that people had built in memory of who knew what over the years. He ran past them, toward the low cliffs that bordered the island.

The ground was rockier here, less green, and the cliffs were pale. Tall waves crumpled against them, wearing them smooth.

As he approached the edge of the island opposite the

hotel, the waves seemed to die down. *Fewer shoals here, probably*, Noah thought, remembering the shallow, submerged rocks for which the Isles were named. The water was calmer and darker on this side. It rose and fell in deep green undulations.

Noah saw a shadow move behind a jutting boulder. He pulled off his headphones. He heard a sharp splash, out of rhythm with the waves, and a crack like breaking bones. A deep cough followed, and a gurgling gasp.

He yanked off his shirt and scrambled down the rocks, scanning the water for the drowning person. He saw a whitish shape under a wave and lunged toward it. There—his arms closed on a soft, struggling form.

A girl slipped in Noah's grasp. She had cropped black hair and silvery pale skin, and—he realized with horror—she was completely naked. He pulled back instinctively and held up his hands to show his innocence.

She stood there glaring at him, fire in her eyes and seawater streaming over her body.

Then her mouth dropped open. "Oh, Goddess," she cried, "where is it?" She dove back underwater, vanishing into the green dark.

Noah stood motionless and dripping, his running shorts plastered to his legs and his socks floating around his ankles like kelp. He had no idea what was going on. And her voice . . . Noah had never heard a voice like that, silky and watery and deep. He hoped he'd have time to explain himself when she surfaced again. He turned away so she wouldn't be embarrassed when she came back up.

He waited for almost a minute and couldn't hear anything behind him. He was starting to worry again when he heard the girl exhale.

"I was trying to save you," he said quickly. "Er, I thought you were drowning."

She laughed, and Noah felt blood rush to his cheeks. He hated that he blushed so red—a family trait. He was glad he still had his back turned.

"Sorry," she said, "to laugh at you, I mean. It's just— I'm a pretty good swimmer."

Noah found himself nodding and pasting an understanding look on his face, even though she couldn't see it. "I'm sorry," he said. "And my name's Noah." He started to turn around.

"I'm just getting my clothes on," she said, and he froze. He concentrated on not remembering what she'd looked like, so suddenly in his arms, all black hair and white skin.

"All right. Turn around."

Noah turned and looked at her. She wore a light blue men's shirt that was far too big; it sagged over her shoulders, and the hem stopped halfway down her thighs. She'd looped a frayed length of nautical rope around her waist like a belt.

She turned and pulled herself up the low cliffs in a few fluid movements. Noah hoisted himself up after her.

She squinted at him, obviously annoyed, her round pale mouth twisted into a smirk. "My name is Mara. For future reference, I don't need saving."

Noah just barely managed to keep from rolling his eyes. "Look," he said. "I was running by here, and I heard splashing and coughing, and I saw you under the water. I just did what most people would do. I didn't think you'd be so nu—er, rude . . ."

"Nude?" she asked, raising her eyebrows. "Because I didn't really need your help with that, either."

"No!" he cried. "I'm sorry, okay? And I didn't know you were, um, clothesless. I get that you didn't need my help, but my intentions were good. You've got to give me that, at least."

"All right." She grinned, and Noah relaxed a little. She sat down at the edge of the rocks, and Noah joined her. "Noah of the noble intentions. Are you named after the sailor?"

Noah didn't know what she was talking about—he'd stopped thinking about her words. Her voice was too distracting, smooth and clear and . . . "Sailor?"

"You know, the flood, all the animals two by two, the big wooden boat with the window at the top for the giraffes' heads to stick out. Noah."

"Right. Yeah, that Noah." Somehow Noah had never put his namesake in the "sailor" category.

He looked at Mara, trying to think of something else to

say. He was distracted for a moment by the water dripping from her hair onto her smooth, pale neck, down past her collarbone and under her shirt. He made himself look away.

"So," he said, thinking it was her turn to be embarrassed, "are you in the habit of skinny-dipping at five o'clock in the afternoon?" He didn't know what gave him the courage to make fun of her like that—it must have been because she already thought he was an idiot.

Her dark eyes flashed. Okay, maybe he hadn't hit rock bottom yet.

"What about you? Am I the first damsel you've rescued, or does your day not start until you've stuck your nose in someone else's business?"

Noah groaned. "Look," he said, "I'm sorry. Again. If I'd known my attempt to help you would be so offensive, trust me, I wouldn't have bothered. But I haven't been here very long, I don't know anyone, and since we've kind of broken the ice at this point . . ." He trailed off, once again surprised at his own bravery. He hadn't talked to a girl his age this much since—ever.

Mara stared at him quizzically. He wondered if she ever blinked.

"I thought we could be friends," he finished with a sigh. He knew exactly how stupid he sounded.

seven

SHOALS

*F*RIENDS. Mara hated how foreign the idea was to her. Still, she didn't know how to respond to this boy, this Noah, who sat on the rocks beside her, still sopping wet, clearly intended for dry land only.

"Um," she said. *Oh, brilliant, Mara. Um.*

"If you want," said Noah. "I haven't had much luck so far, I mean, here . . ." His cheeks glowed still redder.

Mara reminded herself that she had the advantage over him. She knew exactly what kind of person Noah was: a tourist's child, a summer islander, spoiled and boorish and so sheltered that he was years younger than his physical age. He was nothing like her.

Her uncertainty evaporated. She straightened her shoulders. "No."

Noah looked down at the ground, and Mara flinched at her harsh tone. She tucked her hands under her legs. She knew she shouldn't care, but she didn't like hurting his feelings on purpose. "I just mean that I'm not around often. I have responsibilities. I don't have time for . . . anything else."

She met his eyes as she spoke and tried to put as much honesty as possible into her voice. His chagrined smile distracted her, but only for a moment. She *was* being honest, after all. She was very busy. She wasn't even supposed to be here in the first place.

But why had she come, if she wasn't supposed to? Wasn't it precisely for this, to meet someone, to make a friend? Mara tried to be honest with herself, too. It wasn't working.

She looked over at Noah again. He was so out of place here, all red and warm. His hair stuck out in ten different directions, drying in the sun. Mara's own hair was perpetually slick and wet-looking. She cut it short to make it dry faster, but it hadn't helped. Her brother Ronan, so proud of his own long and beautiful dreadlocks, teased her about it mercilessly.

She arched her back and stretched, letting the dry air move over her skin. She had a few hours left before she really needed to return home. Ronan had the younglings, and she wasn't needed to take over until after dark. The Elder was away until morning.

Mara wondered for the thousandth time what they did, Ronan and the Elder, when they left. She warded off her sadness. She knew her family was close to falling apart, but *she* wasn't Elder. There was nothing she could do about it.

"You know," she said, "I actually do have a little time now." She figured she might as well get as much out of her delinquency as possible.

"Oh," said Noah. "Well, good."

They fell silent. The wind was picking up.

"Do you like the hotel?" asked Mara. "It seems like a nice place to stay."

He glanced toward it. "I wouldn't know," he said. "I'm not staying there. I figured you were."

"No, I live here." *Well, around here, anyway.*

"Right. You don't really look like a tourist."

Mara looked away, hunching her shoulders. She'd hoped her clothes weren't that unusual.

"In a good way." Noah groaned. "I just mean that you look like you belong here." He paused. "Maybe that doesn't sound right either. I'm sorry. I've never said anything right in my whole life."

For some reason, Mara smiled when he said that— but she quickly hid the smile away. If there was one thing she could do, it was hide. Concealing a form, concealing a thought—it was all the same.

"Well, I'll believe you're not staying at the hotel," she said, "but you don't exactly look like an Old Shoaler, and you're too young to be one of the fishermen. You're from the mainland, aren't you?"

"Yeah. I'm living with my grandmother for the summer. She has the house on White."

"The keeper's cottage?" Mara had always wanted to explore the lighthouse. If she climbed to the top, it would be the highest above the water that she'd ever been. But it was too obviously occupied, and year-round, too. For years Mara had resented the old woman who refused to go back to the mainland in winter like most of the Shoalers. How she survived the island winters at her age, Mara had no idea.

"I guess," said Noah, "but the lighthouse is automated. She doesn't actually have to *keep* it at all. But you probably knew that."

They talked about the lighthouse, the other islands, and the hotel. Gradually their conversation got easier, losing some of its sparring edge. Mara found herself smiling and laughing, and once she even touched his shoulder — but only briefly, and then she pulled her hand away.

Noah told her about his grandmother and his sister, and about his parents, whom both he and his sister were trying to escape for the summer. "Lo doesn't have a job out here, like I do, but she wanted to get away from them even more than I did. And she likes to draw, and she likes to read, so I'm hoping she'll be all right here while I'm at work, even though she's mostly alone. I don't know what I'll be able to do to help her when I leave for college in the fall."

Mara was startled. "You're leaving your family?"

Noah raised his eyebrows and gave her a funny look. "Aren't you, soon enough?" he countered. "You must be at least as old as I am. I mean —" He blushed again. "Haven't you thought about leaving?"

"Not for a long time." Mara looked out at the ocean.

"I know exactly what I want to do, and it's all here." She thought of the younglings, just waiting for someone to lead them to adulthood. She knew she could do it if she got the chance. If the Elder would give it to her.

"Wow," said Noah. "I can't imagine living in the same place all my life."

Mara listened to him describe the college he'd attend in the fall, and she told him what she could about herself.

"You have *five* siblings?" he cried. "I only have one, and she's more than enough." As soon as he spoke, he looked stricken. "I mean, I love Lo. She's great. But you know." He grinned. One side of his mouth creased under the pressure of his smile. Mara noticed freckles on his nose.

"Five younger," she said. "I have an older brother too, but he's less trouble than the others. Usually." *Noah and Ronan would get along quite well*, she thought. Ronan couldn't wait to leave his family either. A familiar ache twisted in her belly, and she tried not to think about Ronan's plans.

"So, six siblings. I bet you're never lonely."

He was only joking, Mara knew, just as she knew it was her face that looked stricken now.

Noah's mouth opened. "I didn't mean anything by it," he said quickly. "I guess anyone can get lonely out here."

"I love the islands," said Mara. "It's only that — when you said I wasn't lonely —" She paused. "I used to have another sister." Mara hadn't spoken of it, hadn't heard anyone mention Aine out loud, in almost five years. It was strange how dangerous it felt to acknowledge her after so much silence. To acknowledge her absence.

And she'd told a stranger, too. She'd told someone she didn't know at all, someone she certainly shouldn't be able to trust. Mara's whole life was built around hiding, around secrets. She didn't like how easy it was for her to talk to this boy. How much she felt, without any reason for it, that she could trust him.

She stopped talking. She waited for him to prove her wrong.

"Oh," he said. He cleared his throat. "I'm sorry for your loss."

Those words sounded strange to Mara, hollow and wooden, but when she searched Noah's face, he looked truly concerned. Maybe it was just because the word was so apt. Loss. *Aine, where are you?*

She looked at him, and he looked back. They didn't speak.

She looked away. "I should go," she said. "The sun is setting." And it was, or starting to—just a little orange around the edges of the clouds, a shining, a broken path of white light skittering toward the horizon. The islands were beginning to glow.

Noah looked down at his bright, blinking watch. "Oh, God." He sighed, standing up. "I should have been at Gemm's a long time ago." He stretched his lean arms into the sky. When he looked down at Mara, a strange expression came over his face. "Do you want to come? I'm sure Gemm would feed you, and you could meet Lo. I think you and she could be friends."

Mara wasn't sure how to take that, Noah's going from wanting her to be his friend to wanting her to be his sister's. But she got that odd feeling in her stomach again when Noah asked her to come back with him. She must be hungry.

The younglings could eat late tonight, she decided, though they wouldn't be happy about it. She'd worry about that later. A voice in her head whispered that she'd been good enough for one day, one lifetime, that she deserved a little fun. No one would ever be the wiser.

She ignored the other voice, the Elder's voice telling her to be careful, telling her the old stories about outsiders. But the Elder told different stories, too — like the one about the other Noah, with his ship full of animals. He'd saved them and then set them free.

She glanced at her Noah again. Maybe he was like that.

"All right," she said, and found that she was smiling. "I can't stay too late, though."

She walked to his rowboat with him, not at all sure what she really wanted. Her will, her knowledge of herself, always seemed to evaporate when she was on land. Things were so much clearer in the water.

So she sat in his boat and let him push off. This was new, this being in the water and above it at the same time. The currents moved the boat, moved her, but she had no communication with them. She felt isolated and cramped, like a message in a bottle.

She distracted herself by watching Noah. It was strange to see him push against each wave with the long wooden flippers he called oars. They progressed through the harbor at a pathetically slow pace.

"Can I try?" she finally asked.

Noah gave her another sideways look, eyebrows raised. She'd known him only a few hours, but she already hated that look.

"You've never rowed before?" he asked. "You did say you live on these islands, didn't you?"

Mara fought a strong urge to stick out her tongue at him. "Just let me try it," she said, and he handed her the oars. She wrapped her fingers around the wooden shafts and pulled.

Water swirled in circles around the paddles, and she cut easily through each wave. She felt better now, in control of her movement through the water. The boat was a kind of second skin, in its way.

Noah's eyebrows were still raised, but his expression had changed. "I guess you have done this before," he said. "I'll just shut up from now on."

"Fine with me," said Mara, grinning at him, feeling the rush of water underneath them as she rowed.

"I guess the whole 'friends' concept is out the window, then."

"Is that you talking?"

Noah made a horrified face and clapped his hands over his mouth. He looked so different when he joked, his eyes crinkled at the edges and sparkling. His eyes, she saw, were green.

It took only moments to cross Gosport Harbor and the tiny stretch of ocean between Star Island and White. Mara looked over her shoulder and pulled the rowboat up to the shore. Noah jumped out — did he have *any* care for his shoes? — and, wading through the shallows and foam, he pulled the boat onto the gravel with Mara still aboard.

The sound of the hull scraping against the bottom made her cringe. "I've got it," she called, and jumped out, pushing the boat from behind until it rested several paces in from the tide line.

She looked up from her efforts to see Noah recovering from a backwards fall. He had still been pulling the boat when her pushing it had overtaken him.

"You're strong," he said.

"And you're still talking. You'll want to look to that. Now, what's for dinner?"

Mara laughed, and Noah did too. She caught her hand reaching out to take his as they walked inland and pulled it back, mentally smacking herself. What was she doing? Talking so casually with this boy, enjoying his company, *joking*. It wasn't that Noah was particularly interesting, she told herself. People had always fascinated her — otherwise she wouldn't have spent so much time on land this spring and summer. That, she decided, must be the reason—simple curiosity. That was all.

Noah opened the door to the old weather-beaten keeper's cottage, but he didn't go through. Instead, he stood back behind it, clutching the doorknob.

When she stopped to wait her turn, he gave her that look again. "Ladies first," he said.

Mara walked inside, giving Noah one of his own withering looks as she went. She heard him chuckle as he walked in behind her and shut the door.

Inside, the cottage smelled earthy but fresh. Almost everything was made of wood in various stages of wind-worn, gray age. The only color came from ugly green countertops and a pink sofa that slumped next to the stairs.

A woman sat at the table, her back to the door, but Mara recognized her immediately. The invisible link between them hummed and sang with Mara's sudden panic. She tried to quiet her mind, but the moment she'd walked inside, it was already too late.

The Elder turned, her face taut with disbelief. Mara met Maebh's eyes and braced herself for the storm.

eight

SQUALL

I CAN'T believe — to think I trusted you to stay —"
Maebh's chair tipped and clattered to the floor as she stood.
She crossed the room in a few wide steps and grabbed Mara
by the arm. "How many times have I told you?" she demanded. "Goddess, Mara, I need you safe. I need to know
you're safe, always."

The look on Mara's face passed through shock to horror
and shame in a moment, then pulled into anger as fierce as
Maebh's. She met the older woman's eyes. "How can you
say that to me?" she said. "What are you doing here? I know
this place. I can —" She stopped herself, her nostrils flaring.
Noah could have sworn she was about to say she recognized
the cottage's smell. "You can't tell me I'm not safe, Maebh,
when it's so clear you've been here before."

"And your brother? Does he know?" Maebh was shouting now. "And the young —" She stopped and glanced toward Noah. He thought she'd liked him well enough when
they met, but the look she gave him now made him feel like

a kidnapper. He stared down at the floor, his whole body tense.

"Come with me," Maebh hissed. She tightened her hold on Mara and dragged her outside. Noah could hear her shouting again after the door slammed shut, and Mara shouting back, just as angry.

Gemm and Lo sat at the table, their mouths slightly open.

Noah stood speechless for a moment, blinking in surprise. "So I guess they know each other," he said.

He sank down onto the couch and leaned his head back. He officially gave up on making any friends this summer.

"Um," said Lo. "What was that all about?"

Their grandmother sighed. "Just family troubles. In fact, I'm surprised it didn't happen sooner." She shook her head. "But—I think Maebh would rather I didn't talk about it."

"Oh." Lo looked no more satisfied than Noah felt.

Gemm stood and started clearing the table. It looked as if they had just been finishing dinner when Noah and Mara walked in.

"Sorry I'm late, Gemm," said Noah, standing up to help with the dishes. If he arrived this late for dinner at his parents' house, his mother would sulk at him for days.

"Don't worry about it, honey," Gemm said. She started humming to herself as she soaped up the plates.

Noah waited for a passive-aggressive remark to follow, but Gemm really seemed okay with it. He dried the dishes as she washed, then sat down with a plate of spaghetti.

He ate his first bite in peaceful silence, and then realized that Lo was staring at him. No — she was staring at his dinner, wearing such an intense expression of longing that Noah had to look at it again himself, to reconsider how good it looked. But it was just regular spaghetti with Bolognese sauce and a sprinkling of Parmesan. It did smell good, but it was nothing fancy.

"Want some?" he asked.

"No," Lo said, and looked away.

"I can't believe you're still full from lunchtime," said Gemm. "When I was your age, I ate like a horse."

Lo shifted in her seat.

Noah shook his head slightly at Gemm. She raised her eyebrows and then shrugged.

Lo was staring at Noah's food again. He was holding his fork, a bite of pasta in midswirl. He didn't want to move.

Lo made an ugly sound, half groan and half cough. "I'm better now, remember?" she said, standing up. "I went to the doctor, I went to therapy, and I got better. Watch me." She yanked Noah's fork out of his hand and took a big slurping bite. "Would I do that if I were still sick?" she asked. She grabbed her stomach and jiggled her hand up and down. "Christ, would I look like *this*?" Tears started in her brown eyes.

Noah looked down at his plate, once again trapped by his inability to say the right thing. He knew she wasn't better. He knew it. Still, he was glad that at least she looked healthy now, not like the wasted skeleton she'd been two years ago. He remembered the note he'd found on her calendar: *October 20th*, *ninety pounds*. Her thirteenth birthday and her goal weight.

He'd had to tell their parents. They put Lo in therapy, and Mom watched her closely to make sure she ate. They had dinner as a family every night. But when Dad's health insurance stopped covering the therapy, they pulled her out.

And yes, Lo had been eating. Sometimes only celery, sometimes whole batches of cookies, but at least she ate. Noah was happy to see medium- and large-size tags on her clothes when it was his turn to do the laundry, and he pretended he didn't notice when she started cutting the tags off. He made up excuses for her when he heard her get sick in the bathroom. But now, seeing how angry she was, how much she hated her perfectly normal body, he couldn't pretend.

"I've heard you," he said, standing up. "You make yourself throw up. You think you're so smart, like it's this big secret, but it's not." He glanced at Gemm, who was holding out her hand as if she wanted to touch Lo's shoulder. "I thought maybe if we both came here this summer, you'd stop. If Mom and Dad weren't around. I guess I was wrong."

Lo's lips pulled together. "You think this is all about Mom and Dad?" she whispered.

"No, I—" Part of him knew that nothing he could say would be the right thing, but he couldn't stop. "You keep hurting yourself!" he yelled, unable to quiet his voice. "Can't you see that's all you're doing?"

Lo snorted and turned away from him, tucked her chin down, and stared at the floor.

"Lo, honey." Gemm walked into the space between them. "I'm sure Noah just wants you to be healthy." She let her hand rest, finally, on Lo's shoulder. Lo shuddered but didn't move away.

Noah reached out his hand toward hers and she flinched and bolted for the stairs.

"Just leave me alone," she said, pausing halfway up. "I thought at least here—" She ran the rest of the way upstairs and slammed the bedroom door shut.

Noah closed his eyes and rubbed his temples. He couldn't believe how angry he was—angrier than he should have been, angry at Lo for being sick and immature and unable to understand that she was just fine the way she was. Angry at his parents for their constant criticism. Angry at himself for being angry.

Then Gemm put her arm around him. She was tall enough that he could lean against her, and he let her support him for a moment. She patted his back and pulled away enough to look at him.

"I didn't know. I'm sorry I caused an argument, truly."
She sat down on the ragged couch. "Your parents don't tell
me much about you. I wish I'd known."

She looked over at the framed advertisements on the
wall. "I've read about these things," she murmured, "and I
knew a girl or two who did that. Made themselves sick. But
such thinness wasn't important in my day." She chuckled,
her face tired and sad.

Noah looked at her photos, and it was true. The women
in the old advertisements had soft cheeks, curved waists,
flaring hips. None of them would have made it into the
modern fashion magazines his mother and Lo kept around
the house.

Noah remembered the feel of Mara's torso between
his hands, strong but soft, slippery with water. He had to
remind himself of her hostility, her teasing, her bizarre en-
counter with Maebh. No, he told himself, he was not interested. He'd be perfectly happy if he didn't see Mara again
for the rest of the summer—or ever.

What was wrong with him? He should be worrying
about Lo. For the second time that evening, Noah pushed
the memory of Mara's body from his mind.

He heard the couch springs creak, and he turned to see
Gemm walking toward the stairs.

"I'll see if I can talk to her," she said. She smiled at
Noah and lowered her voice. "Maybe you should stay down
here for a while?"

"Right," he said. "I'm not tired yet, anyway. Take your time." He hoped Gemm would get through to Lo. God knew he never could.

Noah settled onto the couch. He heard Gemm opening the door to his and Lo's room, and the faint sound of Lo crying. He tried not to listen in on them. He drummed his hands against the cushions, unable to sit still.

The wind knocked urgently against the windows and doors. Noah remembered a rocky cliff by the lighthouse that stood on the far end of Gemm's island. The waves sprang up and shattered on the gray rocks, with the lighthouse standing, weather-beaten and stoic, above everything. When he'd seen it from the ferry yesterday, he'd thought it was beautiful, but he hadn't had time to visit it up close since he'd arrived.

He creaked the door open, nearly tripping on the uneven jamb.

The air outside was cool, and the wind roughed up his hair. The darkness erased the island's boundaries, breathing infinite space around it. Noah stepped carefully, knowing the island must be smaller than it seemed.

There was a small path between the cottage and the lighthouse, lined on either side with stubs of driftwood. Gemm had said there used to be a whole covered corridor linking the lighthouse to the keeper's cottage. But years ago a storm had blown it all away, and now there was just this path. Crabgrass grew on it, crunching under his feet.

There was seaweed, too, strung in dry bands at the tide lines.

The darkness deepened. The lighthouse was the only shape Noah could make out, illuminated by its own swirling beam. As long as he faced away from it, the whole world was contained in one rotating flash, one circle of light. Everything else was simple, immeasurable darkness.

He moved off the path and edged toward the shore, guided by the sound of the waves. The water rejected the light and glinted it back to him. Moonlight turned the beach gravel to rough pearls under a thin, retracting blanket of sea foam. He sat down.

Noah reminded himself why he'd decided to come here. A summer without his parents — that would be good for him, and even better for Lo, or so he'd thought. He'd known his parents wouldn't let her go away unless he went with her, so he'd been glad to give her this chance. He'd wanted to get to know Gemm better, too. And the internship had sounded so perfect, he would have done anything to take it, even if he hadn't wanted to help Lo get away.

Those had all seemed like good reasons then. But sitting here now, on a cold, damp rock on the edge of a still-colder and damper ocean, on a tiny island miles off the coast of his lifelong home . . . he wasn't sure why he'd come. Things weren't working out as he'd hoped.

He pulled off a sandal and dipped his foot in the waves. Water bubbled around his toes.

A motorboat by Gemm's dock clinked against its mooring. He focused on the sound, and the rhythm of his own breath, trying to forget about tomorrow. It was good, he decided, sitting out here in the dark. There was something satisfying about being so alone, with no one asking anything of him.

Then he squinted at the motorboat and frowned. When he'd seen it that afternoon, he'd assumed it was Maebh's. But of course, if he'd stopped to think, he would have remembered that Gemm had two boats and that this one was the *Minke*. And now Maebh was gone—Mara, too—and the boat remained.

The selkie story whispered back to Noah from Gemm's cottage. He looked over his shoulder. All the lights were out but the one he'd left on in the kitchen. The lighthouse beam flashed over the house and left it behind in an even, wide sweep over the night ocean.

He imagined Mara out there, floating on a dark wave, watching him from the purplish water. He knew from firsthand experience that she had legs, but in his vision she had a long mermaid tail instead, smooth and gray like a dolphin's, undulating in the deep. She smiled, but her teeth were too sharp, too carnivorous, and shiny with venom. Venom he wanted to taste.

Noah shivered. It had gotten cold, and the wind was picking up. The waves quickened, slapping against the shore. He couldn't see the sky, but he felt a storm coming.

He stood up. Mara wasn't looking back at him from the ocean, he knew — she was asleep on another island, not even thinking of him, her legs normal human legs tucked under blankets as she dreamed, her mouth a normal human mouth.

Noah didn't need a mystery or a fairy tale. What he needed, he lectured himself, was to go to sleep, so he could have some chance of not making a total fool of himself at the Center tomorrow.

He turned away from the shore and made his way back to the cottage.

nine

POD

THE younglings were hungry and anxious, and Ronan didn't know what to do. He'd tried to distract them, leading them in races out to the edges of the harbor. He wanted to go hunting. But that wasn't his job tonight — at least, it wasn't supposed to be.

The younglings were too tired to play anymore. They huddled on Whale Rock, their little bellies rising with each yawn. Ronan circled them protectively, spiraling in the water, diving up and down to run off his energy. Bubbles from his angry breaths spurted up to the surface.

He shouldn't even be here. He should have been gone months ago, searching for the others. The Elder had told him he could leave this year, but she'd gone back on her promise just as he knew she would. He'd been grown for almost seven seasons, but he was still trapped here like a youngling. She even refused to let the true younglings mature, and she knew Ronan wouldn't leave while they still needed his protection.

He looked away from the shallow water around the

islands, out into the wild deep of the open Atlantic. They were out there somewhere, the ones who had left him behind. They were waiting for the Elder to lead the younglings to maturity, and then they could all leave these crowded islands and join their family at the other edge of the sea, their true home on the Irish coast.

He still missed them, each one. Now Ronan was the only grown male left. He tried to be father and brother and teacher to the younglings, but he couldn't be everything at once.

He watched Lir and Bram and Nab, still little boys, teasing their sisters even as their own heads sagged with weariness. They needed someone to show them how to be men, and Ronan wasn't up to the task alone. He knew the best thing for them would be to bring them ashore so they could start to grow up. The Elder was supposed to do that for them, but it had been five years since she'd let the younglings go on land. Five years since Aine had vanished.

He felt Mara and Maebh approach. Their minds hummed with anxiety and anger. *What have I done now?* Ronan wondered, before remembering that he was the one who should be angry. They were both late, both irresponsible; yet they still managed to make *him* feel guilty. As always, Ronan was outnumbered.

They finally swam into his line of sight, Mara trailing obediently behind. Large stripers trailed from their mouths — at least the younglings would eat well tonight.

Fear radiated from both of them, Mara's tinted with shame, Maebh's with deep sorrow. Of course, Maebh was the Elder, which meant she could hide some of her feelings. Ronan would probably never know what Maebh truly felt unless she desired it.

In seal form there was only so much he could say, mostly "Food over here" or "Look out!" Instead, Ronan sent curiosity through his link to Mara, hoping she would meet him on the surface later. He sent his indignation, too, just to make sure she'd know how he felt.

He couldn't believe this. He knew Mara had her reasons for leaving the pod from time to time, just as he did, and he respected her privacy as long as she respected his. But she'd never come back so late before, and she'd been found out. Maebh was obviously furious—and scared. And that meant what Maebh's fear always meant: hiding the pod in deeper water, keeping the younglings farther from land. More important, it meant neither Ronan nor Mara would get much time away anymore.

To think he'd hoped Maebh was close to letting go. Mara's carelessness would cost the younglings another season at least before Maebh would let them grow up, and that meant another season of Ronan's staying stuck here on the Goddess-forsaken Isles of Shoals.

Mara nodded at Ronan on her way to the younglings. Maebh herded the smallest toward the fish first, making the stronger younglings wait their turn.

Ronan kept telling Maebh how sparse the fish populations had gotten here, but she'd told him to be patient. That was when Ronan started raiding lobster pots. He took only the best, females with lots of tiny, savory eggs or big males with tender, oversize claws. He liked to imagine the frustrated fishermen pulling up their traps—his favorite, in fact, was a lobster from a pot already reeling up to the surface.

Maebh took over his guard, switching between watching the younglings eat and glaring at Mara. Ronan swam over to Maebh, hoping he could do something to help. She was so angry—even the water seemed murkier around her.

He nudged her flipper gently, for once pretending he was the youngling she wanted him to be. Her black shining eyes flashed at him.

He made a short series of moans and purrs, sounds that meant, *I'm going away.* He nodded toward Mara. In his mind, he tried to show Maebh only concern, not the curiosity and hurt he truly felt.

Maebh huffed out a stream of bubbles, then said, *Come back soon.* Her mind was all fierceness and potential punishments.

Ronan dove and swam to Mara.

She set off before he reached her, tunneling through the water, kelp parting in her wake. They swam toward White Island, far enough from the pod that they wouldn't be overheard.

When they broke through the waves, a storm was brewing. Water swept up and down in jagged crests, foaming around them.

Ronan focused — taking off half the skin was always hard, but he needed to both speak and swim tonight. It peeled slowly at first, from his crown, but then it wanted to separate, to let him turn fully human. Mature selkies mastered the skin's will and their own, denying themselves that temptation, keeping seal form from the waist down. Ronan still had trouble. He had to yank the skin forcibly up his hips and will it to meld back onto his torso.

By the time he sorted himself out, Mara was staring toward White Island, her human arms crossed over her chest. Ronan looked where she looked, but he could barely see through the rain that drove into his eyes. The keeper's cottage was dark; the only thing he could make out was the flashing beam of the lighthouse.

He looked back at Mara, hoping she would explain herself so he wouldn't have to ask questions. She said nothing. The only feeling he could sense from her was shame.

Ronan clenched his fists, wishing he could tear the waves apart. He was sick of it, sick of the silence and sick of waiting around for Maebh and Mara to speak up when he could be *doing* something instead of just hanging on their every word.

"What happened?" he demanded.

She said nothing.

He repeated the question, louder, and she flinched.

When she finally spoke, her voice was quiet and rough. "Maebh found me."

"Found you?" Ronan tried to keep his voice calm. "What were you doing?"

Mara said nothing.

"Well?" he shouted, his control breaking. He wanted her to know how mad he was, to make her realize she'd taken away both their chances at freedom.

"I was on land."

His skins prickled against each other, and a low seal growl escaped his lips. He realized his teeth were bared.

"We had an agreement, Mara." He forced himself to say her name. His tail flicked in the black water.

"I know," she said. "But what about you? Have you honored that agreement, Ronan?"

"Of course." He spat the words at her. "I am Maelinn Ronan, sworn as son to Terlinn Maebh. I keep the honor of my line." He pushed himself farther out of the water so that he could look down at her. "It is you, Maelinn Mara, who have forgotten your honor and your promise."

She shrank from him again. "I know."

He growled again. His spine tightened, and his breath came harsh against his lips.

"I was wrong, Ronan." Mara sounded old when she spoke, tired. "I shouldn't have used your trust against you. I shouldn't have snuck on land."

"You know, don't you, that you endangered the whole pod?"

Mara sighed. "You think Maebh hasn't told me that a thousand times already?" She pushed her short hair out of her face. "Besides, Maebh was on land too. That was how she found me."

"What?" he hissed.

"She was in that cottage." Mara flicked her hand toward White Island. "She was talking to the old woman who lives there." She wrinkled her nose. "I could smell the woman on her when we left. Maebh won't tell me what happened." Her voice wavered.

Under her shame, Ronan sensed suspicion and fear and the quick anger that had been with her since she'd returned. There was something else even farther down, some warmth she didn't want him to notice, but he could feel the pulse of it at her core. He didn't like how good she had gotten at concealing her feelings.

"Maebh is the Elder," he said, to remind himself as much as Mara. "We should not question what she does."

"Yes, but . . ." Mara sighed. "She was so angry when she saw me, but she was frightened, too. More frightened than I've ever seen her."

"Of course she was. You put us all in great danger."

"No. I mean, I did, I know that. But Maebh was frightened for herself, not for me. Not for us." She looked into his eyes. "Whatever she was doing, she was even more frightened that I'd found her out than that I had disobeyed her or endangered the younglings."

The ocean cried out around them. Rain crashed down and blended the waves with the wind. Raindrops needled at Ronan's face.

"What do you do?" asked Mara, finally, raising her voice over the wind.

"What do you mean?"

"You know what I mean," she said. "When I take the younglings and it's your turn to go away, what do you do?"

And what could Ronan say to that?

SEAL

NOTHING," he said. "I do nothing."

Mara wanted to shake him.

"You know it can't be as bad as what I was doing." She sighed. She tried to laugh. It didn't work.

"No. It's not nearly that bad." Ronan looked up at the sky. Mara could hear clouds roiling with thunder, but there was nothing to see. No stars.

"I'm practicing." He shook his head to fling the water off his long dreadlocks. His voice was gruff. "For when Maebh lets me go. When the younglings are grown. I swim out into the ocean, as far as I can go, and then I swim back. I do it again and again, out and back. Soon I'll be strong enough."

"Strong enough?" Ronan was her older brother and the only grown male in the pod. He cared for the younglings, he fought off sharks, and he listened to Mara when she needed someone. What in the world could there be that he wasn't strong enough to face?

"To swim there," he said. "To swim to Ireland."

Mara knew enough not to laugh just then, but she was tempted. "Can't you just . . ." She wanted to say, *just stay with us*, but she already knew the answer to that question. She remembered Noah's eagerness to leave for college in the fall. Why did these young men want to leave their families? "Can't you just take a ship or something? Maebh says that's how our people came here in the first place."

"Maebh did say that." Mara felt Ronan's rage turn away from her, but whether it shifted toward Maebh or their seafaring ancestors, she didn't know. Even the storm seemed timid in comparison to the desperation and anger that rolled off him.

"I won't go back the way they came," said Ronan. "They came over on a slave ship, bound to men who manipulated and abused them." His eyes gleamed, his profile angular against the stormy sky. "That is not the way."

Mara knew as well as he did how horrible those men had been. To steal the selkies' skins, and then to travel so far from their home, still holding them—the selkies had no choice but to follow. Maebh reminded them often of how lucky their ancestors had been when the ship was driven onto the Shoals and the men had drowned. Mara imagined the skins floating up from the shipwreck like oil slicks, shimmering on the water. The selkies who were her many-times-great-grandparents must have collected them joyously, singing into the sky, returning to seal form for the first time in years, and to the water for the first time in months. It was the birth of their pod as Mara had always known it.

But over the years, more and more humans, European immigrants who probably shared ancestry with the selkies' first kidnappers, had taken over the Isles of Shoals. That was why most of the Elders had left five years ago, to seek out a more secluded home . . . and to try to escape the emptiness Aine's loss had left in the pod.

"Why are you so sure they went to Ireland?"

"They must have. Where could they go in America?" Ronan scowled. "Besides, we belong there. Other pods will be waiting for us."

"Still, to swim the whole ocean . . ." Mara sighed. She didn't know how to tell him how impossible it was.

"I can do it," he said, and from the tone of his voice she could almost believe him. "Don't bother yourself about how. I will do it."

She wanted so badly to be a youngling again just then, so she could throw herself into his arms and cry. Why, why did he want to leave?

He sent a cool thread of stability through their link, wrapping it around her confusion. Mara cringed, knowing she'd let her emotions become too open. But she was grateful. She opened her link and let his strength flow into her.

For a moment they were just brother and sister, and Mara could pretend they would always stay like this.

Then Maebh's call sparked into their links. Ronan turned away from Mara.

"Stay here for a while, if you want. I can deal with Maebh." He pulled the sealskin over his head and dove.

Mara knew she shouldn't stay, no matter what Ronan said. She shivered and pulled her sealskin a little higher, up to her ribs. The skin molded onto her belly, warming her from her tail up to her navel. She wrapped her arms over her chest again.

The darkness was almost total, broken only by the beam of the lighthouse and the small, scattered bolts of lightning overhead, not striking down but rumbling inside the clouds, chasing one another.

Mara thought the bright afternoon she'd spent on Star Island must have been in some other life, some other world. She remembered Noah laughing in the sun, his sandy hair catching the light, his skin warm even when he'd plunged into the water to catch her. His strong human hands.

Here everything was cold and wet and lonely.

The storm was quieting. Mara lifted the skin over her head, willing herself into a seal. She kept her feelings to herself as she swam back to the pod.

She was prepared to meet Maebh's anger right away, but by the time she returned, the Elder was herding the younglings to Duck Island for the night. Maebh sent her only a cold twinge of warning. But Mara knew that in the morning, once the younglings were rested and fed again, Maebh would have plenty to say.

They huddled together on one of the rocks around Duck. Scores of seals — true seals, sweet simpletons with no secrets under their pelts — slept around them, along with the large flock of Eider ducks that had given the island its name.

The younglings piled over one another, squirming in competition for the smoothest bit of rock to sleep on. Maebh, Mara, and Ronan took their places around them, guarding them against rogue waves and toothy beasts.

Mara watched her family fall asleep one by one. Ronan snored, grumbling sealy sounds to himself. Maebh slept on her side and reached out a flipper once in a while, as if she expected to find someone sleeping beside her. Mara felt loneliness coming off them in waves — but maybe it was the reflection of her own loneliness, watching her pod fall asleep and feeling, for the first time, as if she didn't belong with them.

She recited the younglings' names to herself as she watched them dream, dusting sleepy flippers over their eyes to ward off gnats. Branna and Innes slept curled over each other as they always did, and Lir, the oldest, stretched himself out by their tails. Bram and Nab slept on their backs, snoring in lighter echoes of Ronan's deep rumbles.

The younglings' smallness, their vulnerability, made Mara's heart ache. She wrapped herself over the edge of the rock.

Every lapping wave slapped loud and insistent against her ears. She turned over and over, trying to get comfortable. Finally, Ronan kicked her and snorted his annoyance, so she stopped.

A sharp pain nipped into her back. She scratched, bothered that some maverick horsefly had made it all the way out to the islands to bite her. She rubbed the itchy spot on the rocks, but it didn't help.

She looked down. Her back smarted, but she couldn't see a bite. Mara scratched again and her sealskin parted in deep folds, exposing a crescent of pale humanskin underneath.

Mara almost fell off the rock. She glanced around, making sure her surprise hadn't woken any of them. No one stirred. With a prayer for her pod's safety, she slipped down into the nighttime green of the ocean.

Though chilly, the surface water was still warmer than the layer of deep Arctic water that lurked beneath it, never warmed by the sun. Mara wanted to stay there, in the in-between. She willed her sealskin back onto her body, but she couldn't make it do what she wanted. Instead, it peeled off more and more, until a human hand slipped free from her flipper and she felt the top of her head opening up. Soon she was looking at the water through human eyes.

She struggled farther down, hoping the cold deep would

remind her who she really was. She might play human sometimes, but she was a selkie, a seal at heart. She refused to be
anything else.

She sang the old songs in her head as she dove:

Morgana, Suleskerry, guide me now
My mother, my father, remember me
I call from the sea to the Goddess
Lead me under, show me the way

Finally she swam deep enough that her human parts
began to shiver and quake with cold, and the sealskin instinctively spiraled back into its snug fit. As soon as her
face knit over with gray velvet, the water flowing around
her felt warmer, welcoming. She sighed with relief.

By the time she had settled herself on Duck Island
again, the horizon showed gray and silver at its edges. Dawn
couldn't be far away. The younglings wiggled and sniffed in
their sleep, chasing dream fish, maybe. Lir had rolled away
from the group, and his tail dangled over the edge of the
rock, almost touching the water.

Mara winced. She nudged the little one back into the
safe center of the pod and wrapped her own body around
the edge.

By dawn she managed to stop crying.

eleven

 H EART

"SWEETHEART," said Gemm, sitting down next to Lo, "we have to talk about this."

Lo uncurled from her fetal position on the couch. She scowled at Gemm's orthopedic shoes. "About what?"

Gemm made the same accusations Noah and their parents and her therapist had spouted all last year: She woke up before dawn, drew or painted through breakfast and lunch without eating anything, then wound up on the couch, circles under her eyes, her blood sugar so low she would almost pass out. Or she ate all day, nonstop, devouring anything in the house, then locked herself in the bathroom with a bottle of ipecac syrup or, once she had built up an immunity to that, just her own fingers.

"How long do you think you can live like this?" Gemm didn't sound as if she were just making a point, even though Lo knew that was the truth. She sounded as if she really wanted to know the answer.

Lo shrugged. She sat up slowly, still looking at the floor.

"Six months more? A year? Two?" Gemm took Lo's chin in her hand, forcing their eyes to meet.

Lo wrenched her chin away and looked down again. "I don't know," she mumbled.

"Yes, you do. Ask your body. It will tell you."

She had to look at Gemm then. The idea of communicating with her body seemed as ridiculous as . . . as talking to a fish. A fish was a stupid creature, low and cold and ugly. Down in the muck, like her stupid fat body.

Gemm took Lo's hand and molded it under her own, keeping her first and middle fingers straight. Lo recoiled from the sight of her bile-worn nails, but Gemm's hold was firm. She guided Lo's hand to her left wrist and pressed the pads of her fingers down on the skin there.

Lo felt her own heartbeat rushing through her too quickly, carrying oxygen to muscles too empty to do anything but tremble. Her throat still stung from her last retch, though she hadn't even eaten yet today. She set her mouth hard, remembering her vow never to cry in front of family. She came close a lot, but always managed to scrape by without tears until she was safely alone.

She felt Gemm's fingers, cool and paper-dry, on her other wrist. "Do you feel it?" Gemm asked.

Lo nodded, scowling.

"That's your heart working too hard, harder than a heart your age should have to work."

Did Gemm's voice break? Lo wasn't sure.

"I often forget I'm not so young anymore," Gemm continued. "My body is the only thing that remembers." She stroked her own cheek, kneading at the wrinkles there. "Every choice I ever made, everything I did, my body kept a record. It tells me stories, and I have to remember to listen."

Gemm touched Lo's chin again, but gently now. "Make your body strong, Lo, and it will thank you, now and when you're an old woman like me." She leaned forward, her voice urgent. "Keep it sick, and you might not live long enough for it to tell you stories."

Gemm wrapped her arms around Lo, and she surrendered, the tears and saliva from her sobs blending together on her grandmother's shoulder.

twelve

 CAUGHT

AINE hated the way he touched her. He touched her as
if her skin couldn't feel, her hair couldn't pull, her limbs
couldn't bruise. He touched her so that even when he was
far away, as he was now, she never felt untouched.

Oh, she didn't think he was trying to hurt her on purpose — he just didn't understand that hurting her was even
possible. The worst was when he made her eat. He stuck
his fingers in her mouth along with the food, just to make
sure it got down her throat. She used to bite him when he
did that, but eventually she understood it wouldn't help.
He didn't feed her for days after she bit, and Aine had never
quite resolved to starve herself. She still thought she might
escape someday.

She couldn't even tell him her name. He called her Hope.
She thought that was stupid. Once he'd caught her, she'd
known better than to hope for anything. Every youngling
heard the stories of captured selkies and their lifetimes on
land. She'd never heard of someone from her pod actually

being captured before, but then, maybe the Elders hadn't wanted to scare them.

Still, she wished she'd known to be scared. She had just been sitting at the top of the beach, quiet and happy, watching Ronan pray. He wasn't quite grown yet, not so tall nor so broad as the other males, but he was strong and kind and serious. As he bowed toward the moon, waist-deep in the water, Aine had thought to herself that no one ever had a better brother than she had in Ronan. He told her stories, saved the fattest fish for her, and even let her nip onto his tail for rides through the water, barreling through the cold depths so much faster than she could swim by herself. The Elders were always distracted, caring only for their own grown-up business, but there wasn't a single day when Ronan wasn't there for her.

At least, not until he'd let the fisherman take her. Ronan hadn't even turned from his prayer; he hadn't even noticed her leaving the beach. He'd just stayed in the inbetween, facing the moon, like the rest of them.

Aine stood, shaking her head violently to push away the memories of her brother. When that didn't work, she backed up into the corner of the little room and ran forward. Her head slammed into the sharp wood at the edge of the window. Black flooded over her eyes.

She came to when a thick, salty trickle slipped into her mouth, onto her tongue. She blinked. She licked the blood away from her lips and sat up, letting the sharp throb on her temple drown out her thoughts.

Eventually the pain faded, and she felt the blood drying on her face. She scratched at it and tiny brownish flakes came off, but not enough to look clean. The fisherman trimmed her nails very short.

Aine licked her hand and rubbed it hard across her cheek, trying to wash the blood away before the fisherman came home. She stared at her little child's hands. The Elders told her taking her skin off would let her grow up, but she hadn't grown a bit since that Midsummer ceremony. Her stupid humanskin felt dry and tight and bulgy, as if her inside parts wanted to grow but her skin wouldn't let them.

She thought maybe if she had her sealskin back . . . but that wouldn't do any good, either. The fisherman had it — she knew he must from the stories; she'd never have gone with him, otherwise — and she knew he wasn't stupid enough to keep it anywhere she'd find it.

Oh, she shouldn't have thought of her skin. Because every time she did, she started to wonder if maybe it had been more than just the skin that had made her leave her pod.

Hadn't she been a little curious? Hadn't she smiled at him when he put his finger to his lips and beckoned? She'd smelled fish on him, and she was so hungry from the days of fasting before the ceremony. Hadn't she thought he'd feed her? Hadn't she followed him willingly from the beach, away from the safety of her pod?

Aine slumped down the wall until she was lying prostrate on the floor. Yes, and yes, and yes. She had gone without struggle. She had stopped fighting him long ago. Even her escape attempts were reduced to ramming her head against the window, and she knew she did that to knock herself out more than anything else.

This, everything that had happened, was her fault. All hers. She didn't deserve to escape.

thirteen

WAVES

MARA took a deep breath, as if her courage were an organ that could draw strength from the air, like her lungs.

Maebh stared at her, pretending patience. Her eyes were narrow and dark. It had been almost a week since they'd discovered each other on land, and Mara clearly couldn't avoid explaining herself any longer. In fact, she could hardly believe Maebh had let her wait this long. Now they stood together in a shadowed cove of Cedar Island, and clearly Maebh would wait no longer.

She wished she knew how to start. Every time she opened her mouth to speak, only anger and accusations sprang to her lips. She knew yelling at Maebh again would just make things worse. She would have to bear it—she would have to apologize if she ever wanted to see land again.

But Maebh was on land too—how can she punish me? Mara shoved that thought away.

She bowed her head to one side, exposing her neck, a sign of surrender even in this human form. "I'm sorry, Elder."

"I should hope so, Daughter." Maebh frowned. "You can't begin to understand the risk you've created."

A growl scratched at Mara's throat, but she refused to let it out. "I know."

Maebh nodded at her. "Go on. You swear never to create such a risk again?"

"What?" The growl escaped against her will. "What about your risk, Maebh? Can you promise to stay away too?"

"I—" Maebh looked toward the lighthouse. "Just tell me: are you willing to give it up, or aren't you?"

Mara's mind rushed toward two separate answers, leaving her torn and battered between them. She needed Maebh's respect, her goodwill, if she was ever to become the next Elder. Maebh would never pass leadership of the pod on to Mara if she believed she would endanger it in any way—no responsible Elder would.

But she couldn't give up the land, the dry air on her humanskin, the bright, sharp colors of sand and grass and sky. She couldn't resign herself to turning human only at the Midsummer ceremonies, to drawing out her life for hundreds of years as only a seal. She knew it was the change that made her age—every selkie knew that. Every time she shifted, seal to human, human to seal, she got a little older. She had been born seventeen summers ago, but she might look eighteen by now, or even twenty. If she kept changing so often, she'd barely live longer than a normal human like Noah.

Noah — remembering him made her even less willing to give up the land. He was the first person she'd ever really talked to outside of the pod. Something about him had bothered her, made her balk at his offer of friendship; yet she'd thought of him often. She'd watched him from the ocean as he'd rowed through the harbor, as he'd run over Star Island in the afternoons. She needed another chance to be his friend.

"No, Maebh," she said, still not knowing if she'd chosen well. "I cannot give it up."

Anger — fear? — flashed through Maebh's link to Mara, but it drained away almost as fast as it came. "Well. I cannot give it up, either." She stroked the soft, black spikes of Mara's hair. "Goddess help us, but we're the same, you and I."

Mara didn't need to speak. Her confusion overflowed, and Maebh's face changed as it poured into her link. She was smiling.

"I know you've been watching the boy. I know you wish to speak with him again."

Mara swatted Maebh's hand out of her hair. "That's not my reason." But something twisted in her stomach.

"You may continue to go on land, so long as you keep to your duties with the younglings —"

"Of course —"

"And so long as you tell the boy what you really are."

Mara stared at the Elder. It was strange enough that

she wasn't punishing her, but this? Maebh must have gone insane. "Weren't we just speaking of—of risks? Maebh, I cannot tell him. None of us can tell any human—ever —what we are." A horrible thought crossed her mind. "Maebh, did you tell that old woman?"

Maebh nodded slowly. "A long time ago. In another case I would agree with you, but Dolores understands. Her grandchildren will, too. They will not betray us."

"How can you know that?"

Maebh looked in Mara's eyes. "That's a story for a different time." She paused, then nodded again. "Dolores and I are always honest with each other, now."

It was almost impossible for Mara to think that the old lighthouse keeper she'd resented for so long could be the same woman Maebh spoke of with such affection. She didn't want to believe it.

Maebh took up her sealskin and wrapped it over her legs. "You think I don't understand," she said. "I know."

She slid into the water and vanished.

Mara looked toward the harbor. A fishing boat trolled its center, helmed by a man with a dark, full beard. And beyond him, a younger man steered a rowboat toward Appledore—Noah. His pale hair glinted in the thin morning sunlight.

She waded into the water and slipped under. She coiled her sealskin over her feet and up her legs and torso. As her two skins melded and stuck to each other, she grimaced. The bones in her legs clicked and scraped and pulled together. She felt her skull shrinking. It hurt.

She surfaced, blinking. Drops of water clung to her whiskers.

She swam toward the boat, pacing herself to the stroke of Noah's oars through the waves.

She remembered Maebh's stories of the sailor Noah. She supposed she must have learned them from the lighthouse keeper. Had the Elder really meant it, that she could tell her Noah what she was?

She remembered more of Maebh's stories, of other humans who had been good to them. The notion of trusting one of them, of telling a human the truth—

I could tell him, she thought. *We could know each other.*

But it was her turn to care for the younglings, and Noah was on his way to work at the Center now too. He would come home to White at the end of the day, at sunset, after he'd gone running on Star.

At sunset she could come on land without guilt, without fear. At sunset she could talk to Noah again.

fourteen

STORY

I DON'T know. I don't know what to say to help her."

Lo stood still on the second stair from the top, at the edge of a puddle of windowed sunlight, listening to Gemm and Maebh's hushed conversation.

"It sounds as if you've helped her already."

"I just wish—" Gemm stopped and sighed. "I wish I could tell her about myself at her age. I wish she could know our story."

"Can't she?"

The urgency in Gemm's next sentence made Lo lean forward to listen better. "What do you mean? Of course she can't." There was a pause, just long enough to be gentle. "I wouldn't tell your secret like that, love."

Maebh's low laugh bubbled through the air. "She already knows most of our secrets, doesn't she?"

Gemm laughed too, softly. "I know she does."

Lo wanted to stay there, listening in secret—but she couldn't quite bear to eavesdrop on her grandmother. They'd started being honest with each other. Lo liked that.

"Gemm?" she called, stepping into the sunlight. The warm wood, worn from so many years of use, felt almost soft under her bare feet.

"Oh—" Her grandmother turned from her seat on the threadbare couch, her long hand still clasped in Maebh's broader one.

"If you want to tell me whatever it is . . ." Lo frowned, trying to find the right words. "I mean, I really want to hear, but I understand if you don't want to tell. But if you don't want me to tell anyone else—I'm good at secrets. I mean, I haven't even told Noah about—um—" She stopped, blushing.

Maebh smiled. Her fingers moved against Gemm's. "It's fine with me," she said, looking at Lo. "It was always the secrets that hurt us, wasn't it? Not the telling of them."

Gemm looked at Maebh briefly, her eyes lined with something sharp and deeply pained. She turned to Lo. She opened her lips, then paused. "It's a secret, true," she said. "A bigger one than you already know. And the worst part —well, it's my part in it, sweetheart. I don't know what you'll think of me."

Lo wasn't sure what to say to that, but Maebh spoke before she could come up with a response.

"We can't control the way they think of us," she said.

Lo remembered the family Maebh had mentioned, and she wondered what they thought of her spending so much time away from them, with Lo's grandmother. That girl with the short black hair Noah had brought home— she was a sister or cousin, surely, and she and Maebh had been so angry with each other. Lo supposed Maebh's family couldn't be an easy one, either.

"All right, sweetheart," said Gemm, moving over to make room for Lo on the couch. "Let me tell you another story."

fifteen

LEDGE

AROUND three o'clock, Professor Foster walked into
the filing room, his hair mussed, his eyes bloodshot.

"Mr. Gallagher." He nodded at Noah. "Come to my office for a minute?"

Noah swallowed. He wasn't sure whether to be scared
or elated. Maybe, he almost dared to hope, he'd get his mentor after all. If he didn't mess it up. If he hadn't messed it
up already. Or maybe that was what was going on—maybe
he was in trouble. What could he have possibly done? He
hadn't had anything the least bit important to do.

He grimaced and followed Professor Foster back
through the lab rooms. As he looked at the research assist-
ants in their dirtied white coats, marking maps of the ocean
floor or attaching tags to the feet of sedated gulls, he felt
twinges of hope. The whole place functioned under a buzz
of seriousness and activity. He just wanted to be a part of
that.

Professor Foster's office was hidden around the corner
from the Center's main hallway. He unlocked the heavy,

solid wooden door and waved Noah in before closing it behind him.

Noah couldn't help but think of the scorn in Mara's black eyes when he'd held Gemm's door open for her. He sat down a little too heavily in the padded chair in front of the desk.

Half the far wall was covered in diplomas, awards, and photographs of the professor with this or that famous marine scientist—even, in one prominent photo, Jacques Cousteau in his wetsuit, smiling next to a very young Professor Foster sporting a brown ponytail. A single small window framed a view of the Thaxter garden and the ocean beyond.

His desk, in contrast, had almost nothing on it. There was a slim, neat file folder, a closed laptop in the center, and a cup with a few sharp pencils. One frame stood there too, but it faced away from Noah. With so many famous people on the wall, Noah had to wonder who occupied the place of honor on the desk.

Professor Foster clasped his hands together on top of the tan file folder. The edges of his mouth curved up in a smile.

"I know I haven't seen you much, and you probably feel like I'm brushing you off," he said. "But to tell the truth, I would like to make you part of the team here, in a more real way than you've been so far." His eyes were light blue behind his glasses, and their corners crinkled with sympathy.

"I can't offer you more money, but I—well, I know ambition when I see it. You're ambitious, Mr. Gallagher. So am I."

All those weekends alone, all those extra classes, his friends back on the mainland spending the summer without him, flickered through Noah's mind. He held in a sigh of relief. "Yes, sir."

Professor Foster looked back at the wall behind him. "You see how proud I am of my accomplishments."

Noah nodded.

The professor's shoulders hunched forward, and he spoke more softly. "However, Mr. Gallagher, soon all this ambition may come to nothing."

Noah blinked. "Excuse me, sir?" He felt as if the professor wanted to let him in on some secret, but he didn't know what it could be, much less how he should react. It seemed that leaving the filing room might be more complicated than he thought.

"You're filing donations now, right?" He didn't pause for Noah to confirm. "You've seen our funding history. You must have noticed how it's drying up."

Noah nodded. He'd tried to avoid noticing, but when he was handling so many grant rejections and quarterly reports, it was hard not to see the general downward trend.

"If we can't get someone—the government, the big pharmaceuticals, commercial fishers—to notice us soon, to notice our work"—he ran a hand through his hair and blinked rapidly a few times; Noah began to understand why Professor Foster always looked so disheveled by the end of the day—"well, Mr. Gallagher, you won't be the only one out of a job at the end of the summer."

Noah nodded. "But, sir, why are you telling me this? What can I do? I mean, of course I'll do whatever I can to help." Professor Foster had said he recognized ambition when he saw it. Surely he had to see how Noah ached and burned to be included in anything that would help him make that leap into really important research.

Professor Foster smiled and folded his hands together on his desk again. "I'm glad you feel that way, Mr. Gallagher. You're too valuable to waste with puttering around in the filing room—don't think I didn't know that when I hired you."

Noah's stomach twinged. *Please*, he thought. *Please.*

"Look, I—there's this ongoing project I've been working on, and I haven't quite found the right assistant for it. It's probably ridiculous of me to turn to someone so young, but you . . . I keep thinking of you in the back of my class, taking all those notes. So many of my college interns, they don't seem to care about anything at all. I—well." Professor Foster cleared his throat and looked down as he polished his glasses with his handkerchief. "How about you come to my house on the mainland sometime next week, and we can talk about the project? You must want to get away from the islands from time to time. What do you think of that?"

Noah's eyes widened. This was so much better than he'd even begun to hope for. "Oh, definitely—I mean, thank you for the opportunity, sir."

"Of course, we do still need someone to sort through all those files . . ." The professor exhaled slowly. "You don't happen to know any organized, eager high school students willing to work for nothing, do you?" He chuckled. "Because nothing is all we've got."

"Actually, sir, I do know someone." It was perfect—Noah knew it as soon as the idea occurred to him. "My sister, Lo, is going to be a sophomore, and she's very organized. She's living on White this summer too. She'd love the job." Maybe a job would give Lo some distraction. Some time outside her own head would have to be a good thing. At least, Noah hoped so.

The fluorescent light above them began to buzz. Professor Foster stood up and tapped it, which only made it louder.

"That sounds perfect," he said, sitting again. "Bring her in with you tomorrow, and I'll get her set up. Then we can move you to the more important things, right?"

Professor Foster held out his hand over the desk.

Noah shook it, trying not to recoil in surprise from the hot, moist skin of his palm.

Walking out into the faded sunshine that afternoon, Noah wondered if he'd finally gotten the internship he really wanted. His new job had to be better than the filing room, at any rate. He'd even gotten Lo a job. But he was surprised to find he couldn't quite focus on any of that. There was someone else he kept wanting to think about, but he steered his thoughts away from her.

He rowed to Star Island. As he stretched and got ready to run, his mind filtered out the buzzing excitement and anxiety he'd felt all day. Running was the only thing that could always do that for him.

The ledge rose at the far edge of the island, straight ahead. He remembered diving into the water, then clutching at something smooth and white — the cool, sweet curve of Mara's waist under his hands, the soft naked O of her mouth, the lilting in her voice.

He ran laps until it was almost dark. Every time he passed the ledge, he convinced himself that he could push a little farther. Every time a wave crashed on the rocks, Noah reminded himself that it was only a wave and not a girl who didn't, as it turned out, need any saving. He was gasping and wheezing with every step by the end of his run, and Mara was nowhere in sight.

No — there *was* someone there, a dark head bobbing in the water twenty feet away. For a moment he thought he saw Mara's shiny black hair, but it was only a harbor seal. It stared at him with large, unblinking eyes.

Noah jogged to the other end of the island, where his rowboat was waiting. He pushed off into the water and glanced around the harbor, pulling the oars with tired, shaking arms. He felt foolish for thinking Mara might have been there again.

The seal followed him. Its dark head faced toward White, bobbing like a buoy in the waves.

He didn't look back until he got home. But the whole time he rowed, straining toward the slowly growing specter of White Island, he could feel the seal's eyes on him, watching.

sixteen

ANCHOR

I WAS young, once too, you know," Dolores began, smiling at her granddaughter.

Lo settled next to her on the couch. She smiled back. "Yeah," she said. "I know."

"I was born here, on the Shoals. My mother was the keeper of the White Island Light for more than thirty years." She looked out the window at the light. "I was lonely sometimes, growing up here — as I'm sure you've been, at least a little — but I loved it. It was like living inside a story."

Dolores felt Maebh's hand slip around hers. She grasped it tight. She closed her eyes and let herself remember.

She spent a lot of time on her own back then, on White Island's pebbled beach or perched up in the lighthouse. She called it the Witch Tower, and she liked to sing out from the top while her beautiful mother lit the beacon. She thought they were both princesses, her mother and she, under a spell, maybe. Living in a story.

Dolores read a lot, to pass the time on the wave-swept

island. Her mind traveled through lots of big, wide, imaginary worlds, while her body stayed in its little isolated corner of the real world. It never occurred to her not to believe in certain things, things that mainland children knew weren't supposed to exist. Things like ghosts, or witches, or selkies.

Dolores and the Shoals suffered through near-constant storms every winter. She couldn't have left her mother's cottage to meet other children even if there had been other children to meet—which, except for the tourists in summer, there usually weren't. She learned to be good at being alone—reading, singing in the lighthouse—but that didn't mean she wasn't lonely.

Her mother had a little red rowboat, just like the one Dolores would lend to her grandchildren many years later. She took it out on spring days when the water turned calm and jewel-clear. With a sandwich and a few novels, she could spend the whole day letting the sea sweetly rock her. She had a little anchor to drop so her mother wouldn't worry.

She always stayed in Gosport, the small harbor between the Shoals. Past the isles, the water got much deeper, three or four hundred feet. Her anchor wouldn't reach that far, and her mother had told her to stay in the inbetween.

She was lounging in her boat one April afternoon, the year she would turn eighteen. It was a sunny day, but she still had to wear a pea coat and hat to protect her from the wind.

April just barely qualified as spring at the Isles of Shoals, and that was by a New Englander's definition.

She had a lovely lunch tucked away in a net sack. The first supplies had come to the Oceanic Hotel that weekend, and Mother always ordered her personal groceries so they could be brought over on the same boat. Dolores had a fresh orange that smelled wonderful and promised the beginning of a summer free from vitamin C tablets, warm bread with a scraping of luxuriously soft cheese, and thick slices of sausage from the pantry. In her hunger that morning she had taken too much, so she decided to use some of the sausage as bait. She always carried a little fishing rod in hopes of catching their supper.

She dropped the hook, line, and bait into the water, tucked the base of her fishing pole between her knees, and opened a crumbling, salt-crusted paperback. She read for hours without feeling time pass at all.

Something tugged at the line, gently, but with enough force that she felt it through her overalls. Young ladies on the mainland wore skirts, she'd been told, but overalls and the wool long johns that went underneath them were essential during island spring.

That tremor on the line puzzled her. Usually when a fish went for the bait, it grabbed on and made a run for it as soon as it had the morsel in its teeth. Not so here—just a little tap, and the line was still again. On the other hand, it seemed like more than a simple bump against a piece of kelp, and the water was far too deep for her line to be grazing the bottom.

Dolores set her book aside and peered into the water. In winter, the Shoals water was darker than it was in summer. The ocean was hibernating, waiting for the sun to come back before it could wake up and sparkle again.

She squinted into the sleepy depths, and at first she saw nothing at all. Then a silvery glint, dim, ten feet down or more, flashed up at her.

It was big, even bigger than the stripers or bluefish that could snap the line and get away with the bait. Dolores's small rowboat began to feel very small, indeed. She felt a bit like the bait herself.

The glint shrank, went deeper, and then it began to rise. Had Dolores been a normal child, she would have been terrified when she realized what she was looking at. As it was, she was simply relieved that it wasn't a shark.

It was a seal, but by the time it emerged from the water, it was a girl.

She was Dolores's own age, or perhaps a little older. Her arms moved subtly in the waves, curved and foam-white. Her face was round and very pale, and her lips were pale too, with a silver shine. Her black eyes were large and wide, a little farther apart than most people's, and her irises in particular were so big, Dolores could hardly see the whites.

Her eyelids were silver gray when she blinked. She had mounds of black hair twisted back against her head in intricate knots and pierced through with spikes of what looked like bone, and with long blue pieces of sea glass. She smiled at Dolores, and her teeth were impossibly white and slick and smooth.

Not knowing how to react, Dolores followed the example of her favorite fairy tale heroines: she offered to share her meal with the mysterious girl. She smiled her most winsome island-girl smile and tore off a chunk of her bread. She held it out over the edge of the rowboat, squishing it in the tight grip of her smooth, still-childlike fingers.

"Want some?" she asked. "It's good."

The girl took the bread eagerly, and Dolores saw that her fingers were slightly webbed. Her palms were even paler than her face and neck. She ate ravenously but stayed perfectly at ease in the water as the waves slipped around her, rocking the little boat. She looked up and around while she ate, at the sky, the lighthouse, the rocks, and the blinding spots where the spring sun dappled onto the water. Mostly, though, she looked at Dolores.

Dolores looked right back, struck at last with the wonder before her. "My name is Dolores Mochrie," she whispered.

A spell had been cast.

"Gemm—" Her granddaughter's voice brought Dolores back to the present.

Lo's back had stiffened. She stared, unblinking, at Maebh.

"Gemm . . ."

Maebh took her hand away from Dolores's and reached for the knitted shawl she'd tucked at her side. It was wrapped around something—her sealskin, silver and dark, with a softness you could feel just from looking at it. She held it carefully, the slight webs between her fingers trembling. Her hands steadied as she took a breath, and then she looked up at Lo. They regarded each other cautiously.

"It is all right," Maebh said. "I'm not so different from you as you might think."

Lo shook her head. "No. It's not that. It's just . . ." She stopped.

"It's so much to take in, I know," Dolores said. "But as I said, Lo—as we said—I think secrets are worse. You'll see."

Lo kept staring at Maebh. She nodded, slowly.

Dolores returned to her story.

They sat in the dark, on the shoreline, their legs almost touching. The edges of waves washed over their feet.

Maebh had followed Dolores to White Island after their shared meal, vanishing behind the cliffs with a dark bundle in her hands and returning wearing a faded, old-fashioned summer dress. She'd murmured that she didn't mind the cold.

The two girls hadn't spoken much, but they stared at each other almost unceasingly. Dolores's mother made small talk with them over dinner, then told Maebh she was happy to see another young person on the islands, and that she was welcome to stay until her own mother wanted her back. She went upstairs to sleep, and Dolores and Maebh became the only waking souls on White.

Dolores had burned with questions all afternoon, but she couldn't ask them in front of her mother. Now that she was alone with Maebh again, though, it was hard to make the questions come.

Thankfully, Maebh spoke first. She smiled and asked shyly, as if the question might be foolish: "Do you know about selkies?"

Dolores shook her head. "Not much. But I believe in them." Carefully, so that Maebh wouldn't notice, she snuck her knee a half inch closer to her new friend's. Warmth rested in the air around her skin, and Dolores could feel it now.

Maebh smiled. "Well, that's something, at least." She sighed and leaned back on her hands. "I don't know what to tell you first."

"Tell me everything." Dolores winced at the sound of her own voice, so much rougher than Maebh's.

"Well, usually, you know, we look like seals. But we can

look like people, too . . . I suppose you know that." Maebh laughed, and for a moment Dolores wondered if the other girl felt as nervous as she did. Her own self-consciousness surprised her, but she told herself it was only that she wasn't used to making friends.

"I don't really know," Maebh said softly, "if we're more seal or more human. The Elders say we're not like humans at all, but . . ." Her voice trailed into silence.

Dolores leaned in to hear her better — and, perhaps, simply to be closer to her.

Maebh's voice came back, a little stronger now. "We have to change form, though, to grow up. When the moon is full, the Elders bring the younglings — our children — to shore, and they teach them the old songs and how to shed their skins. A selkie could live forever if she never changed, but she'd never grow any older, either." She glanced at Dolores, and the look in her eyes made them both shiver. "So far, I like growing up."

Dolores stared back at her, unwilling to move.

Maebh sucked in her breath and looked down. "Besides, the moon ceremony is beautiful, the ritual of it. We spend the whole night dancing and singing and praying to the Goddess — we see her in the full moon."

"The moon?" Dolores had never really prayed to anything before. She'd always preferred magic to gods.

"Oh, yes."

They looked up together. Clouds lay across the sky in stripes, dividing the moon into blurred halves.

Dolores felt wind on her face, in her hair. The clouds shifted, and the moon grew whole. She shivered.

"Here." Maebh's arm wrapped around her shoulder.

"Thanks."

Maebh nodded, silent.

Their legs were touching now, and Dolores could feel a tingle of water around her ankles. The tide was coming in.

They met nearly every evening, after that. They started lighting the beacon together, and Mrs. Mochrie was grateful for their help. They stayed up by the light and talked to each other until Maebh had to go back to the sea.

"Look how dark it is already," said Maebh one evening in the beginning of November. "What's the point of your daylight saving time, anyway?"

Dolores shrugged. "The harvesters need it." She joined Maebh at the window and looked out with her. "Besides, it's not quite dark yet. The sky's got a bit of purple in it."

The beacon rotated behind them. Every ten seconds, they had to squint.

"Are we blocking the light?" Maebh asked. "I don't want to be responsible for any sunken ships."

Dolores laughed. "The light's too strong for our bodies to block it." She nudged Maebh's hip with her own, trying to pretend it didn't mean anything. "You're not a siren, Maebh. You won't sink any ships."

Maebh tilted her head, looking at her friend. "You could be a siren." She gestured over her head. "That long red hair . . ."

"Wait. Are there sirens here too?"

Maebh smiled. "Not here but the Elders tell us stories. They are supposed to be so beautiful, their hair long and bright and curling." She grabbed one of her own black locks and frowned at it, crossing her eyes. "I've always been jealous of siren hair."

"Oh, but I like yours," said Dolores. "Mine's never so shiny. And your eyes—your eyes are pretty too."

She reached up, carefully, slowly. She touched her thumb to the corner of Maebh's eye. Neither of them breathed.

Dolores said, "Tell me more about sirens."

Maebh opened her mouth but didn't speak. She reached down and clasped Dolores's hand.

Before she had time to tell herself not to, Dolores leaned in and met Maebh's open mouth with her own. She felt a smile on the other girl's lips and traced it with her tongue.

The beacon flashed past them, sending its unbroken beam over the sea.

seventeen

RISING

NOAH finally looked behind him once he'd landed at White, but the seal had vanished. He tied off the boat and stepped ashore.

The island smelled fresh in the half-light of dusk. He breathed in deep, imagining the cells in his lungs expanding. The last rays of sun turned the lighthouse's chipped white paint a dripping, translucent orange. The tips of the grasses and leaves lit up like sparklers.

He started walking toward the cottage—he wanted dinner, and to check on Lo—but something pulled him back. He'd never seen the island in light like this before, and it wouldn't quite let him go.

He moved through the twinkling landscape, seeking the cool expanse of the ocean beyond.

White Island had its own cliffs, more dramatic than the ledge at Star. They ran up from the water in rough vertical lines that looked out of place against the organic curve and swirl of the sea. He sat down at their edge, letting his feet dangle. The evening breeze ruffled through his hair.

The seal appeared. It lumbered onto a flat rock at the base of the cliffs, about thirty feet below where he sat. Noah didn't know how he was so sure it was the same seal —but he was. It faced away from him, but Noah was still afraid the seal might notice him watching. He couldn't get over the notion that he was invading its privacy. He swung his legs up and rolled onto his stomach at the cliff's edge, resting his chin on his crossed arms.

The seal's shoulder blades rolled beneath a smooth layer of blubber, its body moving like the swell of the tide. It pulled its head up and to the side, straining toward the sky.

And then its skin began to peel away.

It slid slowly, reluctantly down in wet rolls and furrows. A nascent form emerged: a mop of black hair, round, narrow shoulders, a soft and flexible torso. She rested a moment, the sealskin slipping around her hips. Then, with a flick of her tail, the rest pulled away. Her legs gleamed.

Noah's palms began to sweat. His life rewound to when he was six and Dad told him Santa Claus wasn't real, and that moment was reversed—not erased, but made into a lie. These things were real; they were possible. A heady feeling of infinite magic washed over him. He was the little boy Noah again, the child who believed every star was a UFO coming to take him away.

Selkie. He couldn't stop repeating the word, turning it over and over in his mind like a smooth stone, *selkie, selkie.* Mara was a selkie—what else could she ever have been? No human girl had ever acted as she had with him. It was all part of her supernatural spell, no doubt. He was onto her now.

"Mara!" he yelled.

She jerked around, covering herself with her empty sealskin. She squinted up at him. "Hello," she called back. "Stay there!"

Noah dropped his head between his arms. Too much was happening. He couldn't take it all in.

Before long he heard Mara's soft footsteps behind him. She sat down, dressed in another oversize men's shirt — white this time, with no belt. She wasn't carrying her skin.

"Hello," she repeated.

Noah stared at her.

She sat down beside him. "I'm sorry you found out like that," she mumbled, almost shyly.

Noah snorted. "As if you didn't mean for me to."

"What?" Mara frowned. "I saw you head toward the cottage, so I came here to change. I was going to knock on your door." She looked down at her toes, which, Noah noticed for the first time, were slightly webbed. "I wanted to talk to you."

"Christ, Mara—" He stopped. "That is your name, isn't it?"

She looked wounded. "Of course," she said. "Maelinn Mara, sworn as daughter to Terlinn Maebh." She stuck out her arm in a stiff imitation of human handshakes.

Noah didn't move. "And you are a selkie." He wanted to hear her say it.

"We have many names," she said, "but, yes, that is one."

They sat close together, their legs almost touching. Noah scooted away a little.

"Wait." He remembered Maebh's reaction when Mara had walked into the cottage. "Maebh is your mother?"

"Yes," said Mara. "She is also the leader of our family, our pod. She is the Elder."

"Yeah, well, she doesn't look it." Noah recalled Maebh's smooth, youthful face. "I figured she was your older sister, or your cousin or something."

Mara shrugged. "We age differently than you do."

"Okay, fine," said Noah. "That's not really what I'm having trouble with here." The wind blew too harshly across his hair. He shivered.

He forced himself to look at Mara, to pretend she was only the young woman he'd met a week ago, not some fairy-tale monster who had just shed her skin before his eyes.

Her feet were long and angular, and they turned out from her legs like dancers' feet. Like a tail. Her legs were strong and toned, but smoothed over with the layer of softness he'd felt when he'd first caught her in his arms. Her thighs and torso were hidden under the loose, thin shirt she wore, but his hands recalled the softness there all too well, too.

Mara wrapped her arms around her body and shivered.

Even the translucent webbing between her fingers dimpled into tiny bumps.

Noah realized she was cold. He unzipped his sweatshirt and, leaning over until he could feel the warmth of her breath on his cheek, he draped it around her shoulders.

Tentatively, she smiled at him.

She was still the girl he'd met before. He couldn't deny it, much as his brain balked at the idea. Part of him owned that truth and saw how human she was — even if she didn't fit the technical definition.

"Thank you," she said. "It's always colder this way. No blubber." She patted her stomach. "Well, not as much, anyway." She laughed, and Noah found himself smiling along with her.

It was easy, if he could only let himself go. Noah still wasn't sure if he could, but he decided to try. He sensed that he was working toward something important, and while he didn't quite understand what it was, he wanted — rather desperately — to try to find out.

"You said you wanted to talk to me."

Mara nodded briskly. Her hands moved up to the hood of his sweatshirt and raised it to nestle against her small, flat ears.

"I want to apologize for my behavior last week," she said. "I was rude."

Noah shook his head. "I deserved it. It was presumptuous of me to . . ." He faltered. He didn't want to say *rescue you*; he knew the reaction that would get. "I was being pre-sumptuous."

They sat together in awkward silence. Noah scuffed his foot against the ground.

This was so much easier when she was human, he thought. But then, she had never been human—he'd only thought she was.

"I came to tell you," Mara said, her voice cutting through the whistling island air, "about me. I came to tell you that I am a selkie."

Noah thought he probably shouldn't believe her, but he did. "And Maebh?" he asked. "She doesn't have a problem with your telling me that?" She had certainly seemed to when he'd seen them together.

"Well . . ." Mara hesitated. "You saw us talk about it."

Noah would hardly call that "talking," the way they had crashed out the door like a pair of hurricanes, hollering accusations at each other. He could only imagine how much worse the fight had gotten when they'd gone home to . . . well, wherever they lived. Mara didn't seem to feel guilty, though, as he often did after a "talk" with his parents. He compared their icy silences and passive-aggressive manipulation with the scene he'd witnessed between Mara and Maebh. He decided the selkies' way was probably better.

"It's complicated," Mara said. She sighed. "I think she might understand."

The sky had faded from violet to deep blue. Noah felt the chill more deeply now without his sweatshirt.

"Why don't we go in?" he asked.

He held out his hand, and Mara took it. His sweatshirt's long sleeve flopped down and a breath of warmth drifted onto their clasped hands.

Noah moved his fingers ever so slightly, feeling for the webs he'd seen earlier and hoping she wouldn't notice. They reached only to her first knuckles. He could hardly feel them at all.

eighteen

 SOURCE

MAEBH waited, but Dolores had stopped speaking.

"Should I tell the rest of it, love?" Maebh asked.

Dolores shook her head. "I can bear it. It's remembering, knowing how I hurt you, that's worst."

"No. We're so far from that now. And we wanted to talk to Lo about hurting—right, Lo?"

Lo nodded again, still careful, still disbelieving. She watched them both.

"Love." Maebh pressed her hand over Dolores's. "It is my turn to tell."

In their first winter together, Dolores taught Maebh how to read.

It rarely snowed on the islands, but harsh storms and freezing winds kept them indoors. Dolores offered to lend her novels, but Maebh balked, embarrassed.

"I'll get them wet."

"What?—Oh, I guess you would." Dolores's face colored. Maebh was always having to remind her that she wasn't human, didn't live in a human place. "Well, I can keep it here for you. This door doesn't lock—only the front door does."

They stood together in the narrow corridor between the lighthouse and the cottage, shivering with cold, relishing their privacy.

"Oh . . ." Maebh sighed, searching for some other excuse. Dolores sounded so worldly when she talked about books and the places they described—all the places she yearned to visit someday. It made Maebh feel naïve and homely and a little stupid. She'd hoped Dolores would never find out she couldn't read.

But when she finally told her, Dolores's face showed none of the deep disappointment she'd expected. "I'm so sorry!" she said, as if mourning a recent death. "Well, I'll just have to teach you."

Maebh blushed and looked out the window. It was still raining. The rocks were black and icy, and the ocean was riddled with pockmarks. She hoped her pod had found shelter—then remembered that in seal form, no one minded the cold or the wet. She wondered how she could have forgotten something so basic. Perhaps the Elders were right—perhaps she was spending too much time as a human.

Dolores smiled at Maebh and took her hand, a sensation to which Maebh had almost, but not quite, grown accustomed. She forgot about the Elders.

"Let's go find a book," Dolores said.

Maebh nodded. She glanced around for her sealskin, then remembered it was tucked safely in the rocks on the other side of the island. *As if it would have gone anywhere*, she thought. Still, she couldn't quite bring herself to feel certain, whenever she was with Dolores, that her skin would stay in its proper place.

In the living room, Dolores ran her long, smooth fingers over the musty bindings of the books. "What should we read?" she asked. "These are Mother's, in theory, but this shelf is where I keep all my favorites . . . Oh, I know." She withdrew a thin brown volume and read the title aloud. "*The Journals of Miss Eugenia Humphrey, Lady Adventurer.*"

"No!"

Dolores looked up at her, startled.

"I just think . . ." Maebh cast around for an excuse. She didn't want to hear about the far-off places where Dolores wanted to go, where she could not follow. "How about something . . . something with magic?" In magic, at least, she had more experience than Dolores. She wouldn't feel foolish if they read about her world instead of the human one.

Dolores still looked confused, but she nodded. "Okay, let's see." She grinned and pulled out a much fatter book with a dark blue cover. "This is called *Metamorphoses*," she said. "It was written a long time ago, but people still love it. I think it's the perfect thing to read to a selkie, don't you?" She laughed.

Maebh smoothed her hands over her still-damp hair,

not sure whether to feel happy or embarrassed. "Yes, all right," she said. "That sounds nice." She sat down on the couch, but Dolores shook her head and beckoned her to the door.

"I don't want to bother Mother," she said carefully.

They crept back into the shadowy corridor. Dolores sat down near the window, to use what light they had, and patted the packed dirt floor next to her. "Sit down."

Maebh leaned against the wall and slid to the floor.

Dolores scooted closer to her. "You need to be able to see the pages." She balanced the book on their thighs. One open page lay on her lap, and the other on Maebh's.

"This is an em," she said, pressing her finger under the first black marking on the page. "It sounds like this— mmm." She looked up. "Now you."

Maebh pressed her lips together and echoed the sound. She felt it vibrate in her mouth and stared at the *M* on the page, telling her mind to remember what it meant.

"Good." Dolores smiled at her and slid closer.

Lo was starting to smile now too. She turned to Maebh. "So did you tell her your stories? The selkie stories?"

Dolores shook her head. "Not till later, sweetheart. Not until much later."

Maebh nodded. "We were too busy with our own story, then."

Maebh never wanted to tell Dolores the old stories of selkies and humans. She never spoke of the fisherman, the stolen skin, the captivity. She knew Dolores would never do such a thing to her; she would never hurt her. Maebh didn't think she had to tell.

Every night, swimming away from White Island, she saw their mutual future stretched in front of them like overlapping waves, constant and steady. Eventually, Dolores's mother would retire to the mainland, and Dolores would take over the keeper's duties. Then they could always be together, and if Maebh changed form every day, she could grow old along with Dolores.

Together, they looked forward to the warm nights of the coming summer. Dolores never dared to bring Maebh into her mother's house at night, and it was too cold to stay out for long in humanskin in the winter dark—so while they vowed their love for each other, they shared no further physical affection than occasional embraces and stolen kisses in the lighthouse. Their relationship was a quiet, private one, both because the girls were somewhat quiet and private themselves, and because Dolores told her the world would not want to see them together. She said most humans didn't like seeing two girls in love. Maebh told her selkies weren't like that; they mated and raised their young together in pods, but love was love, and it was something else entirely. She found herself waiting impatiently for summer to return so they might spend a night together on the beach.

But on the first warm night in May — a night she thought she'd ask Dolores to spend with her — the hotel staff played records and drank beer on the Star Island lawns until the sun was almost up. She and Dolores had lain at the edge of the water for hours, waiting for them to go inside. They couldn't quite touch each other, hearing so many others nearby.

And so, when Dolores's mother invited a man to dinner, Maebh wasn't thinking about what that might mean. All she could do was watch Dolores move, watch her speak, watch her eat. The beauty of Dolores's mouth had fascinated Maebh since their first meeting, but now she could hardly bear to look away from it.

"This is Roger," said Dolores's mother when the man came through the door, a bottle of red wine in one hand and a camera in the other. "Roger Delacourt. His mother used to baby-sit for Uncle Jerry and me, Dolores — I'm sure you've heard me mention her — and now Roger's at Star all week, photographing the hotel for the *Times* — imagine that!"

Dolores's mouth opened, and her eyes widened. "Oh," she murmured, "you must travel a lot, Mr. Delacourt."

He chuckled. The sound grated on Maebh's ears. "Yes," he said, setting the wine down on the table and stepping closer to Dolores. "I get around. And call me Roger, please. I hope I don't seem all that much older than you are."

Dolores blushed. "All right, Roger. Could you tell us about your traveling, please? I've hardly been off the Shoals since I was born, and I've never left New England."

"Well, now," said her mother, pressing her hand on Dolores's shoulder, "that's just because you haven't gotten your chance yet."

Dolores smiled shyly at Roger.

It was only then that Maebh pulled her mind away from its dwelling on Dolores's mouth, and she began to wonder about Roger Delacourt.

Mrs. Mochrie invited Roger to dinner every night that week. On the last night of his stay at the Oceanic Hotel, he made an announcement.

He stood up from his chair at the head of the table, a seat Mrs. Mochrie had given up to him from the first, and he raised his glass. "I've fallen in love with these islands," he said, his voice deep and dripping with seriousness. His dull, pale hair stuck out from his head like a false halo, and his green eyes glittered. "I've decided to stay here for the rest of the season, and Mrs. Mochrie has generously welcomed me into her home until another room in the Oceanic becomes available." He nodded toward Dolores's mother. "And so, a toast, to Mrs. Mochrie and her beautiful daughter, Dolores, and to"—he looked sideways at Maebh and gave her a very small smile — "Maebh, her dear friend. I hope we can become a little family this summer."

We were a family before, Maebh thought at him, her back tense and the muscles of her face hard. She stopped wondering about Roger then, and started to worry.

After dinner, Mrs. Mochrie asked Dolores to light the beacon with her. Maebh rose automatically to join them, but Dolores's mother shook her head. "I'm sure you wouldn't want to leave Roger lonely," she said, "and I have something to discuss with my daughter." Her voice was bright and casual, but the fierceness of her expression told Maebh to obey.

Dolores and her mother stayed in the lighthouse for almost an hour. Maebh had ample time, between her awkward spurts of conversation with Roger, to wonder what Mrs. Mochrie might be saying to her daughter.

"Dolores really is a gorgeous girl," Roger said, leaning back on the couch and crossing one ankle over his knee, as if he meant to take up as much space as possible. "I've shot fashion models less striking than your friend, there. She could really make a name for herself on the mainland."

Maebh frowned. "Dolores already has a name."

Roger's laugh cracked across the small room, making her wince. "No, I know. That's not — Jesus. I meant she could be famous, get her picture in magazines, stuff like that."

Maebh had never read a magazine, but she knew she probably shouldn't tell Roger that. Dolores read them, old issues hotel patrons left behind, and she loved to talk about the exotic places and glamorous lifestyles the articles described. But Maebh still refused to believe that Dolores might actually leave the Shoals for the things in books and magazines. She shook her head at Roger. "Dolores likes it here," she said. "She's happy on White. With me."

Roger raised his eyebrows. "That was fine when she was a child, but Dolores is almost a grown woman now—as are you, Maebh. Surely you don't think you'll both stay on these little islands forever."

Maebh's stomach turned, hot and acidic, and she cast her eyes down at the floor. All she could make herself say was, "I don't know."

When Mrs. Mochrie and Dolores finally returned, no one seemed able to meet anyone else's eyes. Mrs. Mochrie busied herself with the dishes, making far more noise and taking far longer than was really necessary.

Dolores stared at the empty seat on the couch next to Roger for a while. Then she sat down next to him, quickly and silently, and gave him a smile Maebh hoped she didn't mean.

"You know," Roger said, sliding his arm along the top of the couch so it rested behind Dolores's shoulders, "I was in Bermuda this spring, shooting a line of resort wear. You'd like Bermuda, Dolores. It's an island too, but much bigger and warmer than this one, and with lots more colors. The beaches there are pink—seashells ground into such fine sand, you'd never guess they once belonged to living things."

Dolores smiled, picturing pink beaches. Maebh thought of all the creatures whose bodies made the sand, all the broken ghosts of shells.

When Roger asked Dolores to come to the mainland with him, Maebh assumed she'd be back soon. They were only going to New York for an audition, he'd said. She hated herself for it, but Maebh hoped Dolores wouldn't get the job.

But she did get it, and the one after that. Maebh still visited White sometimes, over the months that led into another winter, so she could hear the news about Dolores and read her occasional postcard. Not very long after Dolores left, Mrs. Mochrie showed her a department store catalog with her daughter's picture in it. She was in a sweater-set ad, smiling in lipstick the color of a cooked lobster, her eyes lowered. Maebh knew then that Dolores would be gone a long time.

But even as that knowledge sank into the hard pit of Maebh's stomach, settled in the back of her mind, she refused to believe that "gone a long time" was the same as "never coming back." Somewhere between her mind and her belly, those hot, hard places, there rested a drop of faith in Dolores that would not evaporate.

And one day in November, Mrs. Mochrie had news for Maebh. Dolores and Roger were getting married.

Because selkies chose mates but had no ceremony to unite them, Maebh understood marriage only in a vague, story-time sense. To her, marriage was the fate of selkies with stolen skins, something their human captors demanded of them. It was certainly nothing good.

"I'm so relieved." Mrs. Mochrie sighed, leaning back against her kitchen counter. "I was starting to worry about Dolores, growing up on these islands with no prospects to speak of. Thank God for her looks, and thank God for Roger."

Maebh looked away, choking back the immense pressure on her throat.

Mrs. Mochrie looked at her strangely. "Oh, don't worry, dear. I'm sure you'll find someone yourself, soon enough."

Maebh stayed quiet, and Dolores's mother looked down at her hands.

Maebh thought years might have passed in that silence, but she didn't know what to say.

"Oh—I forgot." Mrs. Mochrie strode across the room and began to dig through the small pile of mail on the kitchen table. "Dolores sent you a letter, too. For the life of me I don't know why she sent it here." She held out a small white envelope. "Write her back, maybe, and let her know your own address." She frowned. "Whatever that might be."

Maebh took the letter. "I think I'll go read this now, if

you don't mind, Mrs. Mochrie. I've been impatient to hear from her. I'll light the beacon for you, if you want."

"Oh, thank you, dear." Dolores's mother waved her hand toward the door. She fished a pack of cigarettes from her pocket, lit one, and settled back onto her new pink couch.

Maebh walked outside, closing the door carefully behind her so as not to make too much noise. It was cold and blustery, but she thought she couldn't bear to go through the walkway just now.

She stared at the address on the letter. *Maebh Terlinn, care of Sarah Mochrie, PO Box 7, Isles of Shoals, NH.* So many layers of place, though to Maebh they were only "home." And Dolores had gotten her name backwards.

Maebh tripped over a dry clump of seaweed and fell, scraping her leg open on the rocks. She held back a pained shout, not wanting Mrs. Mochrie to come out and investigate. She stood, straightened her simple blue dress (which had once belonged to Dolores), and kept walking to the lighthouse. She looked at the ground now, and not at the letter.

It was hard to light the beacon alone. The great metal circle that reflected the lamps had to be set in motion, and that required Maebh to turn a huge, heavy crank—one she'd always moved in tandem with Dolores. It felt more than twice as heavy now, and Maebh wondered if Dolores had been pulling more than her share of the weight.

When it was finally done, she lay down on the floor to read her letter. Every ten seconds she felt heat on her skin from the passing lamp, but it didn't last.

Dear Maebh,

I think Mother must have told you about Roger and me, and I'm not sure how to tell you myself if she hasn't.

We're getting married—oh, I know, you won't like that very much. But he loves me, and he says he's going to take me all over the world.

You know, I've only been away from the Shoals for a few months, but it already feels like years and years. The things I did there, the things we did, it's as if I read them in one of Mother's books. Well—not Mother's, perhaps.

Roger calls me Little Mermaid, because of my hair and my being from the Shoals. That makes me think of you, of course. You said I looked like a siren, and honestly I like sirens better than the Little Mermaid story Roger reads to me.

Sometimes I hate myself for leaving you, but I suppose Mother is right. I have to grow up sometime. That's what Roger's given me: a chance at a real grown-up life. I hope you understand.

I still love you. I do. I just couldn't stay.

Yours always,

Dolores

Maebh stuffed the letter crooked into its envelope.

She climbed down the spiraling steps to the lighthouse door and let herself out into the cold. Another storm was coming, and she'd have to put on her sealskin soon to guard herself from it.

She took a deep breath and felt her human ribs expand. She waited for them to crack and implode on the hollow space inside her chest. She thought she'd crumble, her bones becoming a little stretch of pink sand on the rocks. But her body stayed whole.

She scrambled down the cliffs and dug her sealskin from its crevice. She pulled off Dolores's old dress and stared at it for a moment.

She buried her face in the fabric and screamed.

The dress muffled her voice, but she still feared Mrs. Mochrie might come looking for her. She tossed Dolores's letter into the sea and hoped it would dissolve.

She shoved the dress into the rocks and swam away, the sealskin still pulling up over her shoulders.

nineteen

LIGHT

NOAH'S sweatshirt smelled clean and warm, like the wood on Appledore Island's new pier. It smelled like the sun, she thought, knowing that she really had no idea what the sun smelled like.

Her hand in his — that was even stranger than his clothing, his own second skin, wrapped snugly around her shoulders. She felt his fingers move against hers. She wiggled them a little, trying to get used to the sensation.

Noah pulled away. "Sorry," he said. *Sorry for what?*

She pulled her hand up into his too-long sleeve, feeling the downy fleece brush against her wrist. She walked faster. She knew she'd ruined something, and now she just wanted to get inside.

Noah fell into step behind her. The cottage beckoned, and the lighthouse beam seemed cold and alien next to the flickering yellow light radiating from its windows.

Mara reached the door first, and she stepped inside. She saw the same wooden cabinets, green counters, and pink sofa she'd noticed before. A powdery, sweet, human scent drifted over her, one she'd smelled on Maebh many times. The old woman, the lighthouse keeper—Noah's grandmother—stood with her back to the door, bending over a cup of something that smelled really lovely, like hot water and smoke. The girl with the sad face and long black hair reclined on the couch—next to Maebh.

Mara's sudden confusion flashed out through her link before she could stop it. *Does everyone know now?*

Maebh looked up, her face gentle, if unsmiling. Through her link she said all was well. Mara tried to relax.

"Hi, Lo," said Noah as he came in behind Mara.

The girl looked up, startled. She stood slowly. Mara saw that Lo had about the same build that she did, soft and stocky, neither short nor tall. She couldn't help but start plotting ways to become this girl's friend, just so she could borrow some clothes. She was ready to shed her big floppy shirt-dress once and for all.

"It's very nice to meet you, Lo," she said. "My name is Mara."

Lo shot a doubting look over Mara's shoulder. Had Noah been talking about her? Or was it just because Lo had been in the cottage when Mara and Maebh found each other there?

"Is the tea ready, Dolores?" Maebh asked, standing as well. She walked over to Noah's grandmother and placed a hand on the small of her back.

"Yours is on the counter." The old woman smiled, bent her head down, and kissed Maebh on the mouth.

Mara was too distracted by the swell of joy in Maebh's link to know what she felt herself. She looked at Lo, who had calmly averted her eyes—it appeared she knew about this relationship already. Noah, however, seemed more surprised. She heard him draw in his breath. He stepped away from the door, joining Lo by the couch.

"You knew about this?" he asked her.

She nodded, breaking into a wide grin. Noah smiled too.

Mara couldn't help but see how different the two of them looked. Noah was tall and lean, with the unruly, bright hair that kept drawing her notice, a straight, large nose, and green eyes. Lo was shorter, not so lean, with hair nearly as black as her own and brown eyes that were a different shape than Noah's. She thought perhaps Lo might have different parents, like the younglings in her pod.

Lo moved closer to the edge of the sofa when Noah sat down with her. Mara recalled the growing distance between herself and Ronan.

She wanted to slide into the space between them. But the sofa was clearly meant for two, and if she joined them, her hip would press against Noah's. She told herself to stay standing.

Gemm smiled, as if she could tell that Noah knew Mara's secret now. She felt even surer, then, that Maebh really had meant what she'd said. Gemm must have known about selkies for years.

"I think it's past our bedtime." Gemm still wore that knowing smile. She set down her now-empty cup. "Stay up as late as you like—you won't bother us. Good night, loves."

She took Maebh's hand and followed her upstairs.

Mara took a deep breath and looked down at Noah on the couch. He looked back at her, his green eyes steady.

"So," he said. "Are we telling Lo, too?"

Mara shivered. She'd wanted to tell Noah, and she could feel something welling up between them—something like trust. She'd felt it from the beginning, when she'd told him about Aine against her better judgment. She knew, though, as she was sure Maebh did, that it could never be entirely safe to tell their secrets, not to anyone.

But she hadn't been thinking of safety when she'd first disobeyed her Elder, when she'd come on land alone, when she'd first talked with Noah. She already knew there were better things in the world than staying safe. She tried to keep telling herself that.

"Maybe this isn't such a good idea," she heard herself say.

"Isn't it a little late for that?" Noah asked.

"Late for what?" Lo rose from the couch. "What do you think you know that I don't, Noah?"

"I—"

"You're so good at keeping your secrets, you don't think I even notice." Lo's mouth trembled. "You do what you like, and I just sit by and listen, and there's nothing I can do about any of it!"

It wasn't just Lo's mouth, Mara realized; her whole body was shaking. She listened more closely, and she heard something she should have noticed right away: the unsteady, irregular rhythm of Lo's heartbeat.

Noah glared at his sister. "Get over yourself, can't you?" he said, too loudly. "This is more important than your stupid pathological need for control——" He cut himself off.

Lo ran into the bathroom and slammed the door.

Mara was stunned. Couldn't Noah tell his sister was sick? She knew that with his human senses, he couldn't hear Lo's heartbeat as she could. Still, if one of the younglings in her pod had gotten that weak, the signals would be screaming through her link.

A horrible thought struck Mara: maybe humans didn't have links at all. There was no other explanation for Noah's insensitivity. He'd been kinder to her, a girl he hardly knew, than to his own sister.

"That was wrong of you," she said. "She's hurting—can't you see it?"

Noah's head dropped like a chastised youngling's. "Yes," he murmured. "I know. I'm . . ." He sank farther back into the threadbare sofa. "I'm just tired of this."

Mara felt guilty now, seeing the exhaustion spread over

Noah's face. "Tired of what?" She thought about what he must feel: the confusion, the worry for and anger at Lo, the anger at himself for losing his temper. The panic of learning that the world was so much larger and stranger than he'd thought it was.

"Everything's so huge," said Noah, "and so strange. I just wasn't ready for it, I guess. And I didn't think Lo was being fair, and I'm worried about her."

Mara frowned. His words were so close to what she'd imagined he felt. Maybe humans did have links, after all. But they still weren't in the same pod; they weren't family. Mara would never be able to share the same link with him that she did with Ronan and Maebh and the others. She didn't like how much that thought saddened her.

She heard Lo crying quietly in the bathroom, but Noah didn't seem to notice. She knew humans had ears—she studied the looped shells behind his temples—but they didn't seem to work as well as hers. She supposed her human and seal forms had more in common than she'd thought.

Mara walked over to the bathroom door. She pressed her hand against the door frame. "I'm sorry, Lo," she said. "I have a brother too. Sometimes he's horrible." She felt a bit guilty for saying it, as if admitting Ronan wasn't perfect would make him that much more likely to leave. But it was true, and she was sure Lo needed to hear it.

She focused on her voice, the sound humans always found so persuasive, so distracting. She hoped this wasn't the wrong way to use it. "I'll tell you, I promise. Please come out. I was hoping we could be friends." That was true, too.

Lo's crying quieted. Mara heard a sigh like a cramp relaxing. She pressed her hand to the door for another moment, then backed away.

She turned to Noah. He sat with his shoulders slouching and limbs hanging down, as if he didn't have the will to hold them up anymore.

The bathroom door opened, and Lo crept out. Her face was flushed from crying, but she tried to smile.

"I already know," she said, tucking a strand of hair reluctantly behind her ear. "I just—I was just mad Noah didn't want to tell me." Her eyes flicked toward her brother.

Noah stood. "You already know?"

Lo rolled her eyes. "Gemm and I talk a lot while you're off at your job, you know. It's not as if we stop existing when you're not here."

Noah sighed. He started to say something, then stopped and just shrugged. "I know. I'm sorry, Lo." He stepped toward her and touched her hand.

Lo turned toward him and they embraced, the muscles in their arms straining. Noah's eyes closed. Lo's head rested on his chest.

Mara's shoulder blades prickled with sudden desire. Grown selkies rarely touched without a real reason. Mara couldn't remember putting her arms—or her flippers, for that matter—around Maebh or Ronan since she was a youngling. It was an unspoken rule: just as the sealskins kept them hidden and separate and special, so another skin of privacy wrapped around each of them and kept them secure even from one another. Suddenly the lack of a link between humans didn't seem so terrible, if they could have this excess of physical linking in its place.

She thought of Maebh, whose hand had rested so easily on the small of Gemm's back. She wondered how she had learned to share such physical affection with a human.

Lo looked at Mara. "Maebh and Gemm told me about you," she said, "but if you want to tell me too . . . I'd like to know more."

Mara nodded. It was long past dark, and she didn't know how far Maebh's goodwill would stretch tonight. "I'd like to, but I think I need to go home," she said reluctantly. "Why don't you come outside with us?" She pulled Noah's big clean-smelling sweatshirt tighter around her shoulders. She didn't want to delve into her reasons for wanting, so badly, to stay.

Noah frowned. "Wait—" He stopped. She wished he would ask her to stay. But if he did, she might not be able to say no.

Mara smiled at him. "I just thought . . . maybe it would be easier for her to see it. The way you did."

She heard his heartbeat increase. Her own slowed in response, and she inched closer to him, hoping he would catch the rhythm of her relaxed body. At least, the parts of it that were relaxed.

He looked at her carefully. "All right."

She stepped closer, reached down, and took his hand in hers. The hairs on her arms stood up. Her every nerve pushed and prodded her closer to his warmth.

But she stood straight, resisting. She focused on what she needed to say, all the while feeling each pulse through his veins echo into hers. She spoke to Lo, but her eyes stayed locked with Noah's.

"Come with me," she said, "and I'll show you everything."

twenty

RIPPLES

Lo couldn't stop thinking about it.

She'd watched Mara climb down the cliffs beyond the lighthouse. She'd vanished into darkness for a moment, then emerged into a patch of moonlight on the water, holding something soft and dark. She cut gracefully through the waves. When she reached a rock a little ways out to sea, she slipped onto it as smoothly as if she were boneless.

Mara uncoiled the thing she carried, held the edges apart, and pulled it over her feet like stockings. Lo barely had time to notice the crescent tail shape that appeared before Mara's legs were gone, then her hips, then her shoulders and face and hair, all encased in a velvet skin mottled silver and charcoal black. She slipped off the rock, an oblong, slick seal, and was lost to the darkness of the sea.

Noah had laughed. Under his breath, low, not a laugh of humor or derision or even joy. Lo knew what his laughter meant, because she felt the same way. He was laughing just to make some noise at the edge of this unfathomable, infinite ocean.

"Yeah," she said. "I know."

"Do you?" Noah turned to her. "I kind of feel as if I don't know anything. But it's almost nice."

They managed to smile at each other a little. A few minutes passed before Lo could do anything but look at him and know he was looking at her too, and that he saw the same thing she did — someone already long known and loved. Someone familiar.

Then Noah sighed and cleared his throat, and Lo knew that with that sound he was bringing himself back down to earth. "I have something to ask you," he said. "I got a promotion — well, sort of — at the Center, and they need someone to take over my old job."

Lo had inherited enough of Noah's hand-me-downs to know what she was dealing with. This was a bad job, and Noah had managed to weasel his way out of it. Still . . . as good as things had been with Gemm lately, she'd been bored on White. It would be nice to have something to do, some kind of purpose.

In the morning, she found herself stepping into Noah's borrowed rowboat.

Noah took the oars in the stern, and Lo sat at the bow only a few feet ahead of him. He pushed out, and they began the short run across the harbor from White Island to Appledore and the Marine Science Center.

The islands looked different to Lo today, but she

thought that was just because she knew things now that she hadn't before. The waves pricked with light, and yesterday she would have been itching to draw them. Today she wanted to see into the depths, to peel back the skin of the waves and expose the secrets of the ocean inside.

Noah pulled them over the water's surface too quickly. He tied off the boat at the pier and smiled reassuringly at Lo, then grabbed his backpack and set off for the Center's front door at an easy jog.

Lo had to run to keep up. Sometimes his legs seemed twice as long as hers.

The Center was already noisy with activity when they got inside. A boy and girl, each probably a few years older than Noah, huddled on opposite ends of a long desk near the door. Lo saw the girl glance over at the boy. As soon as she turned back to her microscope, the boy looked at her. They back-and-forthed again as she passed, never meeting each other's eyes. Lo laughed under her breath.

Still, she couldn't help but see how pretty the girl was, how poised, how thin. A familiar cramp pulsed through her abdomen. Her cheeks burned. Lo thought she'd done better this summer, had stopped worrying so much about what every other girl looked like. She realized now that there had simply been no other girls to whom she could compare herself.

Except Mara. Lo wondered why Mara, who was pretty

enough and obviously in great shape — she had climbed down those rocks in record time — hadn't hurt her the way this blond girl's beauty did. Maybe it was the way Mara so clearly didn't care how she looked. She always had those old men's shirts on and that tattered short haircut. Weren't mermaids and things supposed to be vain? Maebh must spend hours on her elaborate braids, but Mara seemed to value function over form. Lo filed that observation away to ponder over later.

They'd reached the director's office. Noah knocked on his door, the sound timid, almost reluctant. How scary was this Professor Foster, anyway?

The man who opened the door was tall, even taller than Noah, but not exactly what Lo would call intimidating. His white shirt was wrinkled, his glasses sat crooked on his nose, and he smelled like fish and formaldehyde. Still, his jaw was strong, and his smile was bright. He looked as if he could play somebody's dad on a sitcom.

"Good morning," he said. He fiddled with a large key chain, and a circle of luminous, dark leather on it caught Lo's eye. It glowed with an almost patent shine.

She realized Professor Foster was watching her. She forced herself to stop looking at his key chain, and she smiled at him. "I'm here for the filing job," she said. "Hello."

His eyebrow curled up just a tiny bit. "I thought you were bringing your sister," he said to Noah, his tone still carefully friendly.

Noah's eyes flashed. Lo closed hers; there wasn't much that could get Noah to raise his voice, but this was one of the things that usually could.

"This *is* my sister," he said. Lo had expected him to shout, but his voice was low and icy. "Lo," he said, almost whispering, "meet Professor Foster, the Center's director."

"Of course, of course," said Professor Foster quickly, taking Lo's hand and shaking it. His grip was very strong. "Forgive me, Miss Gallagher. Mixed-race adoption was not so . . . common in my day."

Noah's mouth gaped.

Lo spoke quickly, before her brother had the chance. "I was so glad to get this opportunity," she told Professor Foster, smiling. "I've been wishing for something to organize. My brother never lets me in his room because he knows I'll alphabetize his bookshelves when the impulse takes me."

Noah let out a grumble that could almost have been a laugh.

"Well, we're glad to have you," said Professor Foster, "believe me. I think your brother can explain the filing system to you — right, Mr. Gallagher?"

Lo swept in again. "Of course he can. He already explained a lot this morning." Which was true; Noah had gone over the system in excruciating detail over breakfast, and again in the *Gull*. But even if he hadn't, she wanted to get him away from the director before he said something he'd regret.

She grabbed her brother's arm and dragged him away from the office, down the corridor. "Nice to meet you, Professor Foster!" she called over her shoulder.

"I just need to say something to him," Noah growled.

"No, you don't." Lo sighed. "You really, really don't. You'll just make him mad, and there's no point. He really didn't mean anything by it."

"You're my sister," Noah protested, but Lo could tell his temper was receding. "I don't care what he *meant*."

She shook her head. "I just don't want to get you in trouble, is all. At least not on my first day."

She realized she was still leading him, but she had no idea where they were going. "Is the filing room nearby?"

Noah pointed to a peeling plywood door a few feet away. He opened it for her. It creaked. Everything was dark inside.

"Well, this is it." She saw the corners of Noah's mouth twitch up. As angry as he'd been, Lo could tell he was thrilled she was taking over this job for him.

They walked in together, and Lo groped for the switch. Flat, fluorescent light sputtered over the room.

Noah squinted at her. "Let's go over it again," he said. He moved toward one of the boxes.

"Oh, please, no. You've only explained it five times already." She grinned. "I'm fine, Noah. Go ahead if you want." She gave him one of his old Boy Scout salutes.

He hadn't been a Scout for years, but he saluted right back. He patted her shoulder and turned to leave.

Lo lifted a box onto the ancient desk. She breathed in the smell of dust and old paper. It was no wonder Noah hated this job; he was interested only in things that breathed and moved. He was interested in life.

Lo wasn't so limited. She understood the value of preservation, of detail. She loved the smell of old paper. As she bent over the box and pulled apart the folded cardboard overlaps on top, she imagined the smell of her sketchbooks, a hundred years in the future. She imagined her great-granddaughter sifting through their pages, smiling when she recognized an expression, a setting, the feeling Lo preserved forever in the way she drew the curve of a lip or the sharp frill of a dry leaf. Her art was, in part, a gift for that unborn girl.

Warmth grew behind Lo's breastbone. Yes, even these old papers were important, were beautiful. They let her see the unbroken line of things.

By lunchtime she'd sorted and filed the contents of three and a half boxes. She went to look for Noah in the lab, but he wasn't at any of the stations.

He had her lunch, and she thought with relief that if she didn't find him, at least she wouldn't have to eat. *No*, she reminded herself, *that would be bad*. She thought of what Gemm had told her and reached for her wrist, feeling for her pulse.

She wondered if Noah might have met Mara for lunch. Making a lunch date seemed an incredibly mundane thing for a selkie to do. Still, she and Noah had seemed pretty cozy last night. She'd even worn his sweatshirt, which was ridiculous because it had been at least seventy-five degrees out. Lo scowled.

She wandered outside, looking for her brother and their sandwiches. She circled the Center, unable to find any clues as to where he might have gone. Her belly grumbled at her. She ignored it until it started to clench.

She dug into her purse and found the bag of cookies she'd stashed from Gemm's cabinet. She pulled them one by one from the bag without looking, still walking, still keeping her eyes on the shoreline. She didn't have to think about anything until her fingers brushed the crumbs at the bottom of the bag, and she realized she'd finished all of them.

Her belly clenched again, a different feeling now that she was full, a sort of preemptive wince. But she wasn't going to throw up, she told herself. She was trying to get better again.

She ignored the memories of all the other times she'd thought she'd gotten better. She tried to smile. When her mouth wouldn't turn up, she wet her fingers and dug back into the bag, then sucked on the crumbly sweetness at their tips.

But she could still feel the food settling in her belly, and already her throat widened, ready to bring it back up.

She dodged back into the Center and found the rusty old water fountain by the bathrooms. She took a gulp of tepid water and told her heartbeat to slow down. There was a flycr over the fountain, with a picture of a moon and a star and an advertisement for a dance at the hotel. She tried to focus on reading the words.

Her head swam. She couldn't let herself be sick; she couldn't. She just needed to be alone for a minute.

She retreated to the dark security of the filing room and shut the door behind her, breathing hard. She pressed her lips tight and swallowed, again and again, willing her stomach to be still. Finally it listened enough that she could open her mouth without fear.

She sank down into the old vinyl desk chair, tipped her head back, and closed her eyes. She pushed her fingers into her hair and massaged her scalp. She'd never felt sick like this *by accident* before.

She thought of what Gemm had said. After they'd talked, Lo had thought she'd try harder to stop. She'd told herself she wasn't planning to throw up after lunch today, even though a niggling twinge in her throat told her she might be lying to herself.

She slumped forward, letting her forehead rest on her knees. She locked her hands around the back of her neck.

Someone knocked on the door.

Lo sat up so quickly, her vision crackled into darkness. She gulped from the water bottle on her desk, and her sight cleared. "Hello?"

Noah came in, his face lined with worry. He flipped on the light switch. "Professor Foster saw you," he said. "He told me you looked sick."

Lo waited for him to launch into another self-righteous speech about how she was *hurting* herself; it was *wrong;* couldn't she see what she was *doing*—his usual, in other words.

Instead, he crouched down beside her and placed his hand on her back. "Is it too much, coming here?" he asked quietly. "I shouldn't have volunteered you without checking first. If you want, I can tell Professor Foster you won't be coming in anymore. I can row you home right now." He shook his head. "I was just thinking about myself, I guess. Lo, I'm so sorry."

She felt tears start in her eyes. What had changed, that she could cry in front of family now?

She breathed in the office air, the scent of old paper. "No, I want to stay," she said. "I know I can be good at this job." She smiled at him, thinking that a few minutes ago she hadn't been able to make herself smile. She leaned into the support of his hand. "Besides, we both know I'm better at it than you are."

"True." Noah laughed and slowly stood up. "I just

wanted to make sure you were okay. Take care of yourself."

"You do it pretty well for me."

Noah shook his head. He took a step toward the door.

Lo remembered the flyer she'd seen just before she'd come back to the filing room. "Oh, Noah?"

He turned.

"Do you know about the dance coming up, the one on Star?"

Noah sighed. "You already know more about the social scene than I do," he said, his mouth curving up in a slow grin.

"Well, it's two weeks away. I thought it might be fun to go, but . . ." Lo couldn't believe she was actually going to ask him to come so she'd be less nervous. But no—she wouldn't. She'd think of something else that would make him want to go. At last she wrinkled her nose and said, "I guess I thought you might ask Mara."

Noah jumped back a little. "Why would I want to do that?" He ran a hand through his hair, its tufts rising like bits of flame.

Lo hadn't realized until now how much the island sun had already lightened his hair. She still felt as if they'd just arrived, but Noah's hair and both their suntans meant that summer had already had time to sink into them.

"Why would you want to ask Mara?" Lo rolled her eyes. "I have no idea."

twenty-one

SUNSET

THIS time, Noah knew as soon as he landed on Star that she was there.

He'd come to run again, and Lo had asked him to pick her up at the Center afterward—she wanted to finish filing one more box. She'd really seemed to plunge herself into the internship, and Noah was glad, though he couldn't fathom how anyone could actually enjoy it.

But as he walked up from the pier, he found he couldn't focus on Lo or his job. He didn't know what it was, but some tendril, some invisible thread thrummed in him, and what it told him was *Mara*. More than that, it told him she was nearby, and she was happy.

He stepped around the corner of the hotel, and two cool hands closed over his eyes.

He grinned. "Hello, Mara," he said.

The hands drew away. He turned around and saw Mara scowling, her arms crossed.

"I wanted to surprise you." She shook her head. "But you ruined it."

"I did?"

"You knew I was there!"

"I did." It seemed strange to him, then, how sure he'd been.

Mara's dark eyebrows drew toward each other. "I didn't think you could—"

"I recognized your hands." It was true, after all. He'd seen the webbing.

"Never mind," she said. "I'll surprise you another time."

Noah thought she might reach for his hand, but she turned away from him and set off toward the ledge where he'd first seen her.

"Well, come on," she called, and Noah realized he was standing still, just watching her. He jogged to catch up, and the ground squished under his feet. Had it rained since lunch? He'd been too busy learning the ropes on the equipment the older interns showed him to notice.

The rocky ledge was dark and glassy with wet, and small pools trembled in its hollows. The grass shone with color. Noah had thought his new job would mean more time outdoors, but he'd spent all afternoon in the lab. Maybe he'd ask Lo to eat outside with him sometime. Or maybe . . . "Mara?"

"Mmm," she mumbled, keeping her eyes on a large rock a ways out to sea, stuck through the middle with a jutting iron pole. Noah remembered from the charts at the Center that it was called Whale Rock, named after its resemblance to a harpooned sperm whale.

He sat down with her, but his spine felt so tight, he couldn't lean back or relax. "Do you want to come here with me for lunch sometime?" The question came out in a rush. Noah told himself he was just lonely for some company other than Lo's, but he knew he had the other students for that.

"I can't." Mara didn't elaborate. She just kept staring at Whale Rock. That tendril he'd felt before shrank and faded.

"Oh." It was stupid to feel so rejected. She had been waiting here for him, hadn't she? Didn't that mean she wanted to see him?

He looked out to the ocean with her. Dark shapes circled the far-off rock, ducking under and rising again with the waves. One of them hoisted itself out of the water, nudging its body toward the rusty pole.

They sat there, quietly, for a long time. Eventually Noah felt as if he ought to speak again.

"Are those—" He cleared his throat. "Are they your family?"

"They're my pod," said Mara, with a deeper affection in her voice than Noah had ever heard from someone his age. "My family, although we're not all related by blood."

"Blood doesn't matter." Noah remembered the day his mother picked him up at preschool with six-month-old Lo asleep in the back, tucked into a car seat. They had just gotten back from China that morning, and it was Noah's first time seeing her. She had been so small, so soft and squishy-looking, that at first he'd thought she didn't have any bones. Despite his mother's assurances to the contrary, he'd felt an intense need to protect his little boneless sister. That feeling had never really gone away.

"You're right," said Mara. "Blood doesn't matter. I wasn't sure if humans knew that." She pointed to the largest seal as it chased two little ones in a playful circle. "My older brother." She still spoke lovingly, but Noah heard her voice tighten.

"Conan, right?" He knew she'd mentioned his name the last time they'd sat here and talked.

"Ronan." Mara laughed. "Is Conan a human name?"

"It's my dad's middle name," said Noah.

"Middle name?"

"Yeah, you know, Thomas Conan Gallagher. I'm Noah Christian Gallagher."

Mara cocked her head to one side, considering. "We have two names," she said, "but we are called by the second one."

"Maelinn Mara." Noah rolled it around in his mouth.

"The first part of our Elder's name, and the 'linn' sound, which means 'from.'"

"So you're all named after Maebh?"

Mara nodded. "Now we are. There used to be—well, Maebh wasn't always the Elder. Our pod was once much larger."

He wanted to ask her what had happened. That tendril of understanding had snuck up between them again, though, and somehow he knew she didn't want to talk about it.

"I think Ronan is a human name, too," said Mara. "In every generation, one of our pod's males is given that name. There is a story of a kind man named Ronan who came over from Ireland on the same ship as our ancestors. He lived on the Shoals for many years, but he never told their secret or stole their skins."

"People really do that?" He had a feeling she wouldn't like the question, but he had to ask.

Her eyes flashed. She finally looked at him, but with so much anger in her face that he wished she'd turn away again. "What do you think?" she asked. "Don't tell me you haven't wondered where I leave mine, or what would happen if you took it."

Noah looked back at her. He said nothing.

"I'm sorry." She sighed, and her fingers darted toward him again, just a little, as if she meant to take his hand but then decided against it. She kept looking into his eyes. "You didn't deserve that."

"No, I didn't," he agreed.

Mara stretched out her legs, and one end of the rope

around her waist dropped onto Noah's thigh. She didn't notice, and he didn't want to move lest she did.

The horizon had almost swallowed the sun. The ocean stretched in front of them in cool, thin strips of silver and blue.

"I wish I could come here more often," she said.

"It's okay." He didn't need to hear her explain her rejection.

"It's the pod," she said, looking out at Whale Rock again. "Someone always has to look after the younglings, and there are only the three of us to do it. We take shifts." She counted off the times of day on her webbed fingers. "Ronan leaves at midday, and Maebh always wants nights, though I didn't know why until recently." She laughed under her breath. "So that leaves me with dusk or dawn, and you can see which I prefer. I can come here when the sun is still high, but when it gets dark, I know I have to leave." She picked at a stray thread on one of her too-small sandals. "I can't really appreciate the sunset anymore, because it only means it's time to go."

Noah didn't see what was so wonderful about coming on land when Mara could swim the ocean as a seal, could see and do things he had no hope of experiencing. But he said nothing. He couldn't tell what would make her angry.

They sat still in the darkening air, their breaths coming in and out together. She wasn't looking at him anymore, but he watched her. The wind divided her short hair into swirls and spikes. Her skin glowed even paler in the fading light. This night was warmer than the last time they'd been together, but he still felt as if he could see her breath hanging in the air after each quiet exhalation. The moon rose behind her like a cloudy halo.

Noah remembered something else he wanted to ask. She'd already rejected him once that night, so he chose his words carefully.

"Mara?" He tried to relax, tried to look as if this idea had just occurred to him.

"Mmm," she said again, but this time she looked at him instead of out to sea, and her voice was softer.

"The Oceanic Hotel . . ." He cleared his throat. "They have a party next weekend—for Midsummer—they have it every year, but I guess you probably know that . . ." How to say it? He knew he was babbling. "Lo told me about it. I think she really wants to go, but she's afraid she won't know anyone—"

"I've seen it." She picked up a pebble and passed it from one hand to the other. "I've always wanted to go."

"Oh. Well . . ." *Just go for it*, he thought. "You could come with us, if you want. Um, with me."

She looked down, her lashes casting darkness on her cheeks. "I can't," she said, just as before.

He closed his eyes. *How many times am I going to put myself through this?*

She touched his shoulder.

He shook his head, wishing she'd just let it be.

"I really can't," she said. "Remember? I can only leave the pod during the day. I'm sorry."

She looked at Noah in a way that surprised him; she seemed truly upset that she couldn't go.

She stood up. "It's almost nighttime. I have to leave."

"I know."

She climbed down below the ledge. Noah heard a few pebbles skitter into the water, then splashes and the noise of larger rocks scraping apart, and a soft sound that he thought might be Mara changing.

Then her head peeked above the ledge. "You know what?" A smile slipped across her face. "Yes. I'll go with you." She nodded briskly, claiming some authority she didn't have before. "Okay?"

Noah couldn't help but smile back. "Okay."

Her head dropped down again.

After a few moments he caught the wavering silhouette of a seal in the shallow water, the inbetween space Gemm had described, swimming out toward Whale Rock. Or he thought he did — but he must have imagined it. The water was too dark to tell.

twenty-two

UNDERTOW

MUCH to Ronan's surprise, Maebh asked to accompany him out to sea. He wanted to be alone, but he couldn't exactly say no to an Elder, even one who had lost so much of his respect.

They swam together, slowly at first. Rising sunlight filtered through the water, turning a clear, cool green. They passed over the huge presence of a whale a hundred feet down, moaning its song through the deep.

Ronan swam faster. Maebh paced him easily. As fast as he pushed his flippers through the water, undulated his back, sent sprays of white foam into the air behind him, he still felt her there. She never slowed, never faltered. She sent him a sure and steady calm, pushing it through herself as if it weren't her own feeling but something she wanted to offer to him.

Finally, many leagues out, where they couldn't see land at all, he stopped. They'd swum farther than he ever had alone. Ronan checked in with his body, and the shaky knowledge that he might not have saved enough energy for the return journey flashed over him.

He peeled his sealskin down to his waist. "Maebh," he panted, "hold on."

Maebh circled him playfully, still all seal. Her dark coat blended into the waves, so that sometimes he could hardly see her. When she spiraled, her silver belly flashed.

She swam to him and nudged his shoulder, teasing. She clearly thought they were still racing, still playing, but he'd had enough.

"Stop!" he yelled. "I need to talk to the pod Elder."

She paused and cocked her head at him.

"In case you've forgotten, that's you."

Maebh dipped under briefly, and rose again, half human. The sun was behind Ronan, but he didn't mind making her stare into it.

"We should do this more often." She sighed, squeezing water out of her long, looped braids. "We hardly speak anymore, Ronan."

Underwater, his tail flicked in irritation. "I know."

Her expression softened. "What would you like to talk about?"

He turned away, then shook his head and forced himself to face her. "You." He kept looking in her eyes even as he felt a flash of warning rise through their link. "I—I think the pod needs a new Elder."

"Oh?" Her anger spiked into him like an electric shock. "And who, exactly, should replace me? You, I shouldn't wonder. No doubt you know exactly how a pod should be run."

"I know a selkie who goes on land alone should be punished. I know younglings should be allowed to grow up. They've never changed, not once. Midsummer's coming. Don't you know they need it?"

Maebh's tail thrashed. "Of course I know. I also know what happened the last time we let younglings change."

"This is about the younglings who are still alive, Maebh. Not about Aine."

Their link faded and vanished. Only Elders could build up this kind of wall around their emotions, and now he had to guess what Maebh was feeling.

"I thought we weren't saying her name anymore," she whispered. They hadn't said it in five years—at least, not to each other. But her name echoed through Ronan's mind so often that he'd not even missed its spoken sound.

"Think of Ai— think of her," he said. "Think of how excited she was that night, how happy."

"Until she was taken."

"Yes, but—I mean . . ." He tried to think of how to convince her. "Do you think she would want to keep the others from experiencing that?"

Maebh sighed. "Of course not." Through the waves, Ronan could see her sealskin coiling slowly up her body, another defense mechanism. "And once she comes back, they can all grow up together."

She wasn't listening. "Maebh." He didn't have to work to keep from shouting anymore. His voice was quiet and sad, because that was all he felt. "You can't think she's still alive, not after all these years. One of us would have felt her link."

"Didn't you listen to our stories? If someone's keeping her skin, we can't feel her."

"You don't know that. No one had been taken in generations, before Aine. Stories grow false with time—you've told us that yourself."

But though he would never say so to Maebh, never encourage her false hope, Ronan hoped, too. He remembered the night of Aine's kidnapping with brutal clarity. She'd slipped so quietly out of the link that no one had even noticed, at first—a clean break, painless.

Then the harmony of their singing had broken off into silence as Mara's link was gripped with fear. Ronan rushed to her side, somehow already knowing what had happened.

"She's gone. She—" And Mara collapsed onto the rocks, sobbing.

The Elders called for a search of the island. No one found a trace of her—no one but Ronan. He'd seen the retreating figure of a man, smelled Aine close to him, chased him to the pier—but the man got to his boat before Ronan could catch him.

Even that night, the pod began to collapse. The Elders thought a return to Ireland was the only safe option. They said the Shoals had grown too crowded, that they were almost asking for a kidnapping with so many humans infesting the islands. Only Maebh wanted to wait, hoping against reason that Aine would find her way back. The Elders finally allowed her to stay, to look after the younglings who were too small and weak for the journey. Mara, who was only half grown then and had always been close to Maebh, also asked to stay. Ronan volunteered to stay too, as his penance. He couldn't save Aine, but at least he could keep the others safe. And when they were old enough, he would reunite the pod in Ireland.

But it soon became clear that Maebh loved the Shoals too much to consider leaving. She never let the younglings grow, never allowed another Midsummer ceremony. And every year that they stayed seals was another year Ronan was trapped here, prisoner to his own guilt.

When Maebh spoke, her voice was quiet and worn. "If they grew up," she murmured, "they would all leave. You're itching to go already, and before long Mara will want to leave too." She stared back toward the Shoals. "Eventually, they will all want to leave me."

"Mara won't." How could he make her see? "All Mara wants is to guide the younglings, watch them grow, make the pod strong again. She doesn't care about Ireland as—as the others did. She's your heir, Maebh, and she's a natural leader besides."

Maebh nodded. "Yes, I think Mara could decide to stay. If he—well, if things turn out right, she might grow to love the Shoals, as I do." She shook her head. "But Mara is not ready to be the Elder. She's a child."

"She's less a child than you think she is." Ronan flexed his arms, pulling his anger into his muscles, into his body.

Maebh sighed. "Maybe you're right."

Ronan wasn't sure he'd heard her. "I am?"

"Midsummer is almost here. We can bring them ashore then, on Appledore. The humans have their own ceremony that night, the dance on Star."

"So Appledore will be deserted. We'll be perfectly safe."

Maebh laughed sadly. "Never say that, Ronan." She pulled her sealskin up to her neck. "It will be just the two of us with them, you know. Mara has other plans for Midsummer."

Ronan growled. What could be more important to Mara than the ceremony? He knew she wanted the younglings to grow up as badly as he did.

Maebh shook her head. "Please, Ronan. I'll give you what you ask. We'll have the ceremony. But in exchange, I want Mara to have the night for herself." She touched her tail to his under the water. "We'll take all of this slowly. No matter what you—or she—may think, I'm not ready to give up the pod yet." She smiled at him. "And I'm not ready for you to leave it, Firstborn."

Ronan knew he'd won and that he should be happy. The younglings were finally getting their chance, and in a few seasons he could leave to seek out the others. But as he pulled himself into his skin once more and followed Maebh home, all he could feel — through Maebh's link and within himself — was loneliness and fear.

twenty-three

LINE

SOMETHING was wrong.

Noah had felt it all evening, ever since he'd boarded Professor Foster's boat. He'd thought that being invited to this dinner meant the professor considered him special and was excited about working with him. But the man he'd hoped to call his mentor had been tense and distracted for the whole ride to the mainland.

When they reached the harbor, Professor Foster pulled back on the *Celia Thaxter*'s throttle, still not speaking. The boat slowed, and the engine quieted. He steered into the berth without a word, until he abruptly tossed Noah a line. "You know how to tie her off?"

"Yeah." Noah jumped onto the dock. He looped the rope around the nearest cleat in a figure-eight pattern. When he looked up, Professor Foster was waiting for him.

"Still takes you a while, doesn't it? Practice makes perfect, Mr. Gallagher."

His house was only a few minutes' walk from the docks, a drab box of brown-painted wood on a block of bright blue and white houses. His lawn was green and immaculate, but the rose bushes along the walls had wilted into gray brambles.

"Well," he said. "Welcome." He held the door open for Noah and trailed him inside. But the words sounded false, and Noah couldn't quite bring himself to feel welcome.

After showing him into a small dining area, Professor Foster vanished into the kitchen. He was gone a long time.

Noah looked around at the dark wood-grain walls that seemed to loom in on the room, making it even smaller and darker. He missed Gemm's powdery whitewash.

He told himself he should be excited to be here. "Chill. Nothing's wrong," he lectured himself, not realizing he'd spoken out loud until Professor Foster appeared in the doorway.

"What was that?"

"Nothing, Professor."

"Oh, none of that, now. We're not at work anymore. I hope you can—" He stopped.

Noah waited. Then he heard it too: a loud thump from upstairs, like the sound of someone falling.

"Ah . . ." Professor Foster's face was white. He set down two plates, full of steaming, yellow risotto and sautéed chicken. Noah's mouth watered, and he breathed in the smell of butter and wine. He and Lo had had an early lunch, and now he was almost starving.

"It's only my dog," said the professor. "Just a moment, Noah."

Noah's hands itched to pick up his fork, but all his parents' training in manners wouldn't let him. He kept still and watched the professor leave.

A door opened and shut upstairs.

"Quiet!" He heard a loud smack. Something scuttled across the floor. "I need you to behave," Professor Foster said more quietly. "I have a guest now. I'll come back later." There was a pause. "Good girl."

Professor Foster entered the dining room again. He held a bottle of wine, half emptied, and two glasses. "I'm sorry about that. Wine?"

Noah's parents and Gemm sometimes let him have wine with dinner if he asked. "Um, okay."

The professor poured a small glass, then a larger one for himself, emptying the bottle.

Noah took a sip and tried to pretend he liked the bitter taste. He cleared his throat, hoping that when his voice came out, it would sound adult. "Um, what's this project you've been working on? The one you wanted to tell me about?"

Professor Foster frowned, nodded, leaned back in his chair. "Right. Well, as I might have mentioned in class, Noah, I've been particularly interested in seals for several years now."

Noah gagged on his bite of smooth, buttery risotto.

"Seals?" He thanked whatever luck he had left that his voice didn't break.

The professor nodded. "You might remember, a few years ago, all the stories that were circulating about sharks: how they never get cancer, how certain of their hormones mimic antioxidants, how even their skin cells can ward off carcinogens?"

Noah nodded, feeling grateful for all the weekends he'd spent in the UNH library instead of out with his friends —not that his friends had ever been much for going out, either. His thoughts turned to the Oceanic's Midsummer party, and Mara. Just because he was new at this, he reminded himself, didn't mean he was entirely destined for failure.

Focus. "I remember, sir."

"Well, unfortunately, shark DNA is too differentiated from our own to be much use to us in treating human cancers. But there are all manner of wonders in the marine world, as you are of course aware. What we really need is an animal with closer evolutionary ties to human beings." He tapped one long finger on the table. "A marine mammal. A seal, for instance."

"More like humans." Noah felt his face grow cool and damp. He wasn't sure he wanted to eat any more.

"Exactly." Professor Foster looked past Noah, already caught up in the stream of his own thoughts. "Did you know that several cultures even tell stories of seals that can shed their skins and turn human? Irish, Scottish, Icelandic, Faroese . . . Their lore is remarkably similar."

He glanced away, then back at Noah. "I can tell you, if you like."

Noah took a breath. "I'm sure it's fascinating."

Professor Foster smiled. "It's well enough." He looked away again, at the ceiling — at nothing, as far as Noah could tell.

"There's always this man, a lord, or sometimes a prosperous tradesman, a fisherman. His town is by the sea, of course. These stories always come from coastal communities.

"One day the lord finds a sealskin on the beach. It's large and beautiful, and he takes it with him, thinking he could make a coat of it or some such thing. But as he walks home, he begins to hear soft footsteps behind him.

"He turns and sees this gorgeous woman standing there, staring at him, with more love in her simple dark eyes than he'd ever seen in a human woman's — not that he wanted for female company, powerful as he was. But this woman, she looks at him as if he's her god.

"So he invites her to come home with him. She does, and they marry, and soon they have children." Professor Foster stopped for a moment, thinking. "They have beautiful children, and they love them. The lord always keeps the sealskin in his chest, to remember the day he met his wife — his true love, what have you." He waved a hand absentmindedly and cleared his throat. "But one day, one of the children is going through the lord's chest, and he finds the skin. He brings it to his mother and asks her what it is.

"The woman snatches the skin from her child's hands and runs, never so much as looking back. She's lost to the sea—a seal-woman, a selkie. She abandons her husband and children, just like that. She leaves them. They never hear from her again."

The professor's fingernail tapped an erratic ting against his empty wineglass. "So. The moral of the story. If you find a sealskin, you damn well hold on to it. Even those primitive cultures knew sealskins were precious, life-changing." He took a breath. "The end."

Noah realized he'd been staring at his fork. He exhaled, slowly, carefully, and looked up. He wondered if the selkie stories would follow him wherever he went now. He wondered if Professor Foster had ever heard another version.

He was suddenly desperate to change the subject. "What kind of dog do you have, Professor?"

"Oh." He frowned. "She's just a mutt. I adopted her."

"That's nice." Noah tried to smile.

He shrugged. "She needed a home."

Noah nodded absently. Professor Foster's version of the story had disturbed him—had frightened him, even. How could he take the fisherman's side? But Professor Foster was a man Noah had wanted to work with for years—a good man. He just knew the wrong version of the story.

He heard another thump upstairs.

"Damn it!" Professor Foster dropped his fork. "The stupid bitch is always knocking over my furniture." He stood up. "Next time I'm going purebred." He chuckled.

Noah listened to him walk upstairs again, then heard another smack, another warning. The dog was silent.

When Professor Foster came back downstairs, his face was grim, but he smiled when he saw Noah. "Now let's start talking about the projects I can give you. I'm glad you're here," he said.

Noah wished he could say the same.

twenty-four

CUSP

Ronan shoved his sealskin down his hips and tugged on the human clothes Maebh had given him. They belonged to that boy — Noah — and they were much too narrow and long for him. They smelled like the big building on Appledore and all its dead fish and strange chemicals. His biceps bulged in Noah's constricting sleeves, and Ronan had to roll up the jeans' cuffs.

"Pathetic," he huffed, flexing his arms and hearing the shirt's seams rip. He knotted his dreadlocks with a loose strip of cotton he tore from one of the sleeves. He rolled the pant cuffs once more, wishing they weren't so tight around his calves.

He watched the humans leave the Center one by one. Mara said they'd leave early today for the idiotic human ceremony she was going to on Star. Ronan clenched his fists. The way humans danced, it was practically sacrilege. They had little grace and no focus, and it seemed they danced only to impress one another. He couldn't imagine why Mara would want to join them, unless it had something to do with the skinny, weakling human whose clothes he'd borrowed. Maebh's *insisting* she go was even harder to accept.

He wondered if the Elder was enjoying this, knowing Ronan had gotten what he wanted, only to lose his sister's company during the ceremony. When she told the younglings, he had been flooded with relief. He remembered Mara's first ceremony, only a few seasons after his own, and the happiness he'd seen on her face after her first change. Ronan wanted her to see that happen to the younglings; he wanted her to finally understand the joy that helping to raise her had brought him. He wanted her to be there when they saw the younglings' human faces for the first time.

Unbidden, his mind brought up the image of Aine's smile when she first shed her skin.

His fists tightened again. Mara should be at his side tonight, to witness this, to help keep them safe.

Instead, she was with a human. Ronan had pointed out the irony of it to Maebh, that Mara was the one leaving instead of him. But when a great wave of sadness had flooded into him through their link, he'd stopped speaking.

Maebh had quietly asked him to prepare the island for the younglings' arrival. Then she'd turned, covered herself in her skin, and swum to where Mara and the younglings played out beyond Whale Rock.

What preparing the island meant, he wasn't sure. They chose Appledore for the ceremony because all the humans would flock to Star that night for the dance, and Appledore offered a rocky inlet that couldn't be seen from the hotel. It was a harsh shore without soft grasses or sand, but on this first ceremony since Aine's kidnapping, Ronan put safety before any other concern.

He found thirteen broken bottles in the tide pools between the rocks. He ripped the other sleeve off Noah's shirt, wrapped it around his hand, and gathered up the glass shards. They glittered green and brown and sharp. He took the glass to the other side of the island and scattered it on the lawn, where it would have a better chance of slicing open some human foot. It was their trash, after all, and he thought they should pay for their own sins.

There were small pink crabs in the tide pools too. Ronan picked up one the size of his palm and crushed its shell between his teeth. He sucked out the soft, quivering flesh. He gathered more crabs into one large pool for the younglings to eat after the ceremony. They had been fasting for two days, to make the change easier, and shedding their skins would make them hungrier still. The crabs would be the first food their human mouths would taste.

Ronan heard voices coming from behind him, near the Center. He abandoned the tide pools, not wanting to draw attention to the ceremony site. As quickly as Noah's too-tight clothes would let him, he loped away from the shore and up the hill, toward the Thaxter gardens. He often saw humans admiring the flowers, and he hoped his presence would go unnoticed there.

He walked past the rosebushes, breathing the pollen-fogged air. The colors and textures in this land garden were dry and boring, nothing compared to the kelp forests he roamed underwater. He leaned over to feign interest in a yellow rose, and the humans let him be. They walked past him to the pier and filed into a motorboat that groaned under their weight. They pressed together, laughing, and the boat puttered toward Star.

Ronan walked cautiously up to the Center itself. He skulked past the front door, peered into windows, and listened for movement inside. He cased the building three times before he could assure himself that it was empty, and by then it was nearly dusk. The sun and its harsh light were fading, and soon the moon would rise. It was almost time.

Ronan returned to the inlet, still listening for humans. He heard only the whispers of the water and wind, and the faint bustle of preparation coming from Star.

The ocean doused the last shreds of sunlight. Standing in the blue darkness, Ronan sent Maebh his confidence that the island was ready, that she could bring the younglings here. A few minutes later, he saw a trail of smooth dark heads bobbing toward him through the water.

After five years of silence and stillness and hiding, the pod would start to grow again. He was ready.

twenty-five

LINK

LO insisted he wear the dark blue button-down shirt, and Noah eventually complied. "Indigo," she called it. Mom had gotten it for him on his last birthday, but he'd never worn it. Noah liked neutral colors that let him blend in with his surroundings. Or green. Green was okay. But this color was rich and dark, and the fabric wasn't quite normal—it had a sort of fine-woven sheen to it. It made him stand out. He'd never considered that a particularly good thing.

I don't know, he thought, standing in front of the bedroom mirror. He pulled at his cuffs, trying to smooth out the wrinkles in his sleeves. The color made the white T-shirt he wore underneath look very, very white. He knew that just meant he'd spill something on it soon.

"Hi, Mara," he said to the mirror. He rolled his eyes at himself. He tugged at his shirt one last time, straightened his shoulders, and left the room.

The downstairs looked empty, but Noah heard the discomfiting sound of girlish giggles coming from behind the bathroom door. He recognized Lo's high-pitched titter, which he'd always found so annoying, and the aged softness of Gemm's voice. The third laugh, low and even, he'd only recently come to appreciate.

He glanced at his watch. Even prom hadn't made him this nervous. *You're being stupid. It's just a party.*

"Are you out there, Noah?" The bathroom door muffled Gemm's voice.

"Just waiting on you," he called back. Had he sounded too impatient? He walked to the sofa and sat down, trying to figure out whether his legs would be crossed or uncrossed if he were actually waiting there patiently.

Gemm came out first, her gray hair done up in curls and old-fashioned red lipstick on her thinning lips. "I taught them a few tricks," she said, beaming. She glanced a bit wistfully at her old advertisements on the wall, but she kept smiling.

Lo followed Gemm. She wore a loose, boxy black dress that made her look like a walking rectangle, and her hair was slicked back in a low bun. She'd contoured her eyes with thick, dark liner.

Mara appeared next, smoothing her hands over her short hair. Her dress was a deep, liquid green, with a flowing skirt that ended just at her knees. Her cheeks and forehead were tinged with silvery pink, but he couldn't tell if it was makeup or a blush.

Gemm winked at her, and Mara sighed and slowly

turned around. The back of her dress dipped very low, exposing the smooth curve of her back. Nestled in her hair was a headband of small, creamy pearls.

Gemm leaned over Noah. "You're staring," she whispered.

He felt his face burn.

"Did you see her stockings? It's sort of an inside joke."

Mara wore fishnets. She glanced at Gemm and plucked at them with nervous, manicured fingers.

Noah raked his hands back through his hair, then panicked when he remembered Lo's careful styling from that afternoon. He looked over at her, and she grinned.

"It looks better your way," she said.

The compliment brought Noah back to himself. "You look nice too." He took a step toward Mara. "And you look, um, really nice." *Gorgeous*, he thought, but he was pretty sure he shouldn't say it. They had never said this was a date —he didn't know if selkies even had dates.

"Thank you," she said. "Dolores and Lo were so kind, lending me all these things."

The three of them exchanged smiles. Noah felt a brief surge of jealousy for the easy bond they shared.

"I can't see why you won't wear the sash, Lo," Mara said. "It looked beautiful."

Gemm nodded.

Lo's lips trembled, and Noah feared they were in for another hunger-induced tantrum. But she looked from Gemm to Mara, inclined her head, and said quietly, "I guess I could try it again."

Mara clapped and went back into the bathroom, returning with a shining length of white silk.

Gemm took it from her and wrapped it around Lo's waist, tying it in a cascading bow at the back. She retreated a few steps and smiled.

It was startling—instead of a fabric box, Lo was wearing a real dress. A pretty dress.

"Very Audrey Hepburn," Gemm said. "You look lovely —you all do."

Mara sighed. "I wish I could dress like this more," she said. "I love your clothes, Lo." She spun around, and her skirt lifted out in a circle.

Of course the dress must be Lo's, Noah realized, though he couldn't remember his sister ever wearing it. He hoped Lo would be glad she and Mara wore the same size. Mara looked so beautiful—maybe it would help her.

Lo seemed to have the same thought. She stroked the sash at her waist and smiled.

She glanced up at the clock. "We'd better go," she said. "It started half an hour ago, I think."

Noah had watched the hotel staff preparing for the dance through his bedroom window. The sun was just setting when he came down, and the tent had lit up with the firefly yellow of a thousand tiny string lights. He could hear a subwoofer's heavy thud carrying all the way across the harbor.

Lo grinned. "Well?"

"Don't let me keep you, lovelies," said Gemm, hugging each of them in turn.

They boarded the *Minke* and puttered over to Star Island. Noah tossed the line to a waiting deckhand and jump-stepped onto the pier.

Before he could turn around, the deckhand offered to help Lo out of the boat. She looked startled but took his hand with a shy smile.

Noah offered his own hand to Mara. She shook her head and jumped from the boat to the pier in one fluid movement, sliding her fingers into his only after she found her own footing on land. Noah was still trying to get used to the idea that she took his hand only when she didn't need it.

The air glimmered with the last traces of twilight. Noah glanced behind him and saw Lo engaged in a halting, blushing conversation with the deckhand.

He, on the other hand, couldn't think of anything to say to Mara. She held his hand, and she smiled at him expectantly, but he couldn't think of a damn thing to say.

It was, thankfully, too loud to talk much once they got inside. Pop music blared at them through speakers hung in each corner. A wooden floor covered the mostly level ground, but the dancers still leaned against a slight tilt down toward the shore. The lights glowed with lurid, alien colors: orange, red, purple. Balloons clustered above everyone like a spoonful of caviar.

Not many people were dancing yet. Most milled around, eating from bowls of pretzels and candy or drinking punch dispensed from a small silver fountain.

Noah clicked the pieces of his courage together. "Mara —want to dance?" he called over the music. He turned around, but she was gone.

He panicked, then saw her on the other side of the tent, already dancing. She grabbed Lo's wrist and pulled her away from the deckhand, twirling her into a quick-spinning whirlpool of shining fabric. They laughed as they circled each other, hands clasped, arms stretched out tight. They looked as if they'd always been friends.

Noah looked down at his own hands, which felt suddenly empty. He walked over to the table, lifted a glass of punch, and swallowed it down, but he couldn't shake the empty feeling. He looked for Mara again; she was still with Lo. The two girls kept collapsing with laughter.

He told himself he should be happy they were having a good time together, but he still turned away. He didn't realize he'd been chewing his thumbnail until his teeth cut too far and he cringed, clenching his thumb into his fist so it wouldn't bleed.

He heard the music change, the dance beat fading into a slow guitar sparkle. He felt a tap on his shoulder.

He turned and saw Mara, her face still flushed with laughter, her chest moving up and down as she regained her breath. "Hello," she said.

He cleared his throat. "Hi."

"So." She touched his hand. "Do you want to dance with me?"

Noah looked down. He could feel every single cell of his skin where her finger touched it. He looked back up.

"Well?" Mara's brows arched into dark crescents.

He smiled, nodded, and took her hand in his.

Many of the dancers had retreated to the tent walls, eyeing potential partners warily, so they had the dance floor almost to themselves. Mara stood in front of him, waiting.

Tentatively, he touched the deep curve of her waist, sliding his other hand into hers.

Her arm wound around his shoulder. She smiled at him, and they moved into step together.

Noah took a deep breath. He focused on the music, wondering if his feet could follow the rhythm. The song's beat was slow and clear. After a few moments he relaxed enough to look into Mara's eyes, to notice how she felt against him.

She smelled like water and nighttime air. The front of her dress brushed his shirt, and it took all his willpower to pretend he didn't feel it. Her hands were cool, her torso warm where it touched his.

She pressed closer to him and rested her head on his shoulder.

He slipped his hand around to the small of her back. His thumb came up just over the edge of her dress, and the soft warmth of her skin met his. He closed his eyes, moving his thumb slowly up and down. He felt her shiver under his hand, and heard her sigh.

The song ended.

Then Mara pulled away, and the front of Noah's body grew cold. She wouldn't meet his eyes.

He felt suddenly angry. She was the one who'd pulled him in close, leaned on him while they danced, sighed against his ear. Now she stared at the floor, her head turned away, her eyes down.

He was sick of her contradictions. They needed to talk.

"What did I do?" he asked.

She looked up at him, finally. Her lashes were thick with water.

She dashed out of the tent.

Noah stood still for a moment, staring. He shook his head and ran after her.

Outside, the air was still and hot. The flames of cheap torches flickered around the tent's edges. He chased her until they'd left most of the light behind.

She stopped, spun, and faced him. "Why would you do that?"

Noah gaped. "What?"

"To me. That." Her eyes narrowed to black slits.

He stepped toward her. She backed away.

"Mara, come on." He stepped again, and she retreated again. "Mara, please, what did I do?"

"You—we—" She looked away. "You linked with me. I could read your feelings."

Oh, God. Noah didn't know what linking was, but he definitely didn't want Mara to know what he'd felt with her in his arms—his thoughts hadn't exactly been chaste. He cringed, thinking of what she now knew.

"I'm sorry." How was it this girl made him apologize so much? "I didn't mean to do anything, I swear."

She turned away, covering her face with her hands. "I didn't think we could do it. I didn't know if you could even do it at all."

"Do what? Mara, please, explain. What is linking?"

She placed her hand on his chest. "Don't you feel it?"

"No, I—"

He stopped. He could feel his own heartbeat, but another beat behind it too, not quite in sync, faster than his own. His chest was warm where Mara touched it. He chased his own thoughts from his mind, listening for that *other* that he could barely sense at the edge of himself.

He sensed fear, doubt, heat . . . and entwining everything was a desperate, thrilling connection. They were just like his feelings, but somehow he knew these were not his own.

"Yes," he said, amazed. "Yes, I can feel it, a little." He frowned—when he spoke, his sense of that *other* in him went away. "Maybe—" He pressed his own hand over hers. He listened to her breath and matched it, inhaling and exhaling when she did. "I'm not sure . . ."

He stood still, listening, struggling. He could hardly hear the music anymore, but the sound of waves rushed loud in his ears. He closed his eyes, waiting for something he wasn't sure he'd recognize.

"Here." A surge of determination crossed over his heart, and Mara closed the distance between them, pressing her lips to his.

Their heartbeats rushed through his body. His arms circled around her, just so he could keep himself from falling.

twenty-six

GONE

THE kiss was not brief, but it ended sooner than Mara would have liked. Noah pulled back, gentle but firm, his link a tangle of confusion and joy. His pale eyebrows were raised and his mouth was still slightly open, with just the shadow of a smile at its corner.

When she smiled back, he pulled her in again, and she had to close her eyes, the better to taste the human sweetness of his mouth. She leaned into his kiss and could not help but slip farther into the link.

Then a rush of fear burned through her, scouring her bones and searing her skin. Her mouth broke away from Noah's in a scream that at first she did not recognize as her own.

"What is it?" He reached for her.

She backed away, her body pleading with her to run toward the shore, to dive and swim and find her pod—find Ronan, whose pain and fear called more strongly through her link than anyone else's.

She ran toward the ledge where she always hid her skin, slipped over the wet rocks, and crashed into the water. She felt scrapes sting her limbs, but she ignored them. It was only her humanskin, and soon she would be a seal.

She tried to cry in a seal voice, but her human mouth couldn't make the sounds. She was still plunging her arms into the rocks, searching for her skin, when Noah reached her.

"Mara—oh my God, Mara, what's wrong?" He climbed down into the water with her. He grasped her arms and drew her toward him.

Mara stared at him, then down at her hands. The webs between her fingers were torn from the rocks, some split down to her knuckles and pulsing blood.

She pushed at the fear screaming inside her. It wasn't just Ronan—the whole pod was rent with horror and pain. It was coming from Appledore.

Mara flinched. All at once, she knew what had happened.

She clenched her bloody fists, yanked her arms away from Noah's grasp, and dove into the water.

"Mara!" Noah's calls grew faint, blending into the rush of waves.

Lo's dress sagged heavy on her as she swam. She kicked off the high-heeled shoes and tore a few strips off the skirt before giving up. She'd move faster if she thought only of swimming.

But swimming was painfully slow in this form, without a seal's flexible spine or powerful flippers to help her. In her humanskin the water was cold, so cold.

Her link pulled her toward Appledore, and she told herself to keep moving, struggling with her long and useless human limbs.

Her feet touched bottom and she ran, spray swirling and splashing around her. Lo's headband fell over her eyes, and she pushed it back. Her chest heaved, unused to such a constant need for oxygen.

She thought she'd find the whole pod on the shore, but Ronan stood there alone. He wrung his sealskin in his hands and paced the rocks like a trapped beast.

"Mara!" he hissed, running to her through the shallows. "What took you so long?"

"I—" She gasped, willing her breath to slow. "I tried to come quickly. I—"

He cut her off. "It doesn't matter." His gaze jumped past her, out to the open ocean. "It's too late now."

"Oh, Goddess—please, Ronan, just tell me."

"It's Lir." Ronan met her eyes. The guilt in his link hit her like a rogue wave. "He's gone."

"Gone?" The panic Mara had felt before vanished. Everything inside her grew empty and blank. Even the air seemed grayer, drier. Her skin turned cold.

She thought of the other younglings. For their sake, she

managed to collect herself enough to speak, enough to act. "And the others?"

"Maebh has them, out by Whale Rock. We haven't told them everything yet, but of course they know he's gone." Ronan's shoulders convulsed. Thin tracks of salt shone on his cheekbones. "I can't believe I let it happen again."

"It wasn't you." Was it Maebh's fault, for insisting she go with Noah and Lo to the dance? Was it her own, for agreeing? She couldn't tell now. She tried to send Ronan comfort, but all she could find in herself was that suffocating blankness. She had no comfort to give.

She tried to think of something that would stop him from drowning in his guilt and panic, something that could occupy him and help the younglings. "Go hunting. Find something for them to eat. They're hungry, and probably even more frightened than—well, than we are. They need you. I'll stay here and look for answers. Just because Aine—" The name caught like a barb in her throat and she could not speak. She took a deep breath and tried again. "I'll stay here. Go to the younglings, Ronan."

She felt him wanting to protest. She straightened herself to her fullest height and stared him down with all the authority of an Elder.

A growl rumbled in his throat. She kept looking into his eyes.

He lowered his head and nodded.

She felt almost triumphant for a moment. Then she remembered why they were doing this, and she hated herself for taking pleasure in besting Ronan.

"You're right," he said. They both knew the younglings' safety was the most important thing to him.

He wrapped his sealskin over his shoulders and waded into deeper water.

Mara watched him swim away. She reached out with her mind, searching for the pod. The Elder was easy to find, and the younglings' links surrounded hers like a faint halo. They were all frightened, of course, the little ones overwhelmed with exhaustion and hunger. The guilt flowing through Maebh was like the pressure of another ocean.

Mara pushed the doors of her link closed, knowing she couldn't think with the pain of her pod filling her senses.

It seemed impossible that another of their number was gone.

No, she told herself, *not gone. Taken*. This was a kidnapping, just like Aine's.

Mara's jaw tightened. She wished she could be both seal and human when she found Lir's captor, so she could wring his neck and sink her sharp teeth into it at the same time.

She waded through the shallows, flaring her nostrils to sniff out Lir's scent. She could smell every member of her pod, their excitement during the ceremony, the rank scent of their adrenaline and fear when they realized Lir was gone.

A faint smell of rot slithered up from the pools between the rocks. The tide was at its lowest now, and the corpses of trapped fish and mollusks were exposed to the air. It was a richly sour smell, so close to the scent of food that for a moment Mara found it appealing.

Her stomach turned. Behind the rising smell of decay in the water, she caught Lir's scent. It was faint, much fainter than the scents of the other younglings. She frowned and concentrated only on Lir, wondering why she could smell only a vague hint of him.

Then she knew — it was because he hadn't been afraid. Whoever had kidnapped him must have taken his skin quickly, so Lir would have been immediately under his thrall.

Mara clambered over the loose rocks at the shoreline, following the youngling's trail. It wove around a few boulders, but was otherwise straight. It led to a large, spindly bush behind the ledge.

Another smell, stronger than Lir's, lurked there. Mara knelt down and touched her fingers to the ground, then raised them to her nose. This scent was human — and familiar, though she couldn't tell why.

She smelled fish, dead, but not rotten like the fish in the tide pools. Scents specific to humans flooded her nose: plastic, chemicals, and air grown stale in closed rooms. There was a trace of fresh wood, too, the wood on the new pier at the other end of Appledore.

Mara's blood flinched in her veins. She knew why the smell was familiar. Noah's scent was younger, cleaner, but these trappings—the fresh wood, the echoes of the Center—were always on him.

"Goddess." Mara sank down on the rocks.

She'd told Noah everything—how could she have been so stupid? She'd described the ceremony, how it could only happen at Midsummer . . . She'd even told him how Aine had been stolen. He knew about the power a stolen sealskin bestowed on its thief.

Lo's soaked, muck-stained dress draped cold over her skin. She grabbed at its heavy folds, wanting to tear it off so she could return to her sealskin and her pod.

Then she stiffened in horror. She'd left her skin on White, near Gemm's cottage. Noah would know where to look for it.

She sprang up and ran into the water. She crashed into the waves, kicking against them as if they were assaulting her. She opened her pod links wide, letting their pain pour in and drown out her sole, unbearable thought: if Noah wanted to take her skin, she was already too late.

twenty-seven

SEARCH

Lo felt a rough hand on her shoulder. She turned and saw Noah, his face pale and stricken.

"We're leaving." He spoke between deep, ragged breaths. "We're leaving now."

"What?" Lo pried his hand off her. He'd never grabbed her hard like that before, and she knew he didn't mean for it to hurt. But it did, and she was angry. "Noah, I'm sorry Mara left. But I want to stay."

He glared at her.

"I'm having a good time." She looked around the semidark tent, at the faces of the people she hardly knew but had somehow managed to dance with. She realized, saying it, that it was true. "I want to stay."

Noah made a sound in his throat that was almost a growl. "You don't understand. We're leaving."

"But . . ." Lo looked back at her brother, and she felt her anger dissipate against her will. His eyes were wide and restless, his gaze darting around the tent, and his pants were drenched to the knees with seawater. "Oh, all right."

He took her arm again, only a little more gently this time, and led her out of the tent.

Outside, she pulled him to a stop. "Tell me what happened."

Noah shook his head. His whole body seemed to sink under some weight. "Mara's gone." He took a breath. "She ki—We were outside, and I was trying to get her to tell me why she was upset, and she was starting to tell me, but then . . ." He raked his hands back through his hair and groaned. "It was as if an electric shock hit her, or something. She ran down to the water, and she was digging through the rocks. Then her hands started bleeding, and when she couldn't find her skin, she dove into the water and swam away, and it's so dark—God, I have no idea where she went. We have to go look for her."

Lo touched his arm. "Okay. But if you don't know where she went, and it's so dark, it won't do any good just trolling the ocean for her, right?"

Noah's eyes, which had been almost welling over with tears, now dried and flashed. "Christ, Lo, I can't just sit around and do nothing—"

"No. That's not what I'm saying." She just wanted him to calm down. Seeing him on the edge of panic like this was almost physically painful. She was ashamed to admit to herself that a few months ago she wouldn't have cared about his distress . . . but things were different now, and she wanted to help him. "I meant that we should go back to Gemm's, since that's where Mara's skin is. I bet she just went back there."

Noah closed his eyes. He laughed. "Yeah, except that actually makes sense." He ran his hands through his hair again. "I'm such an idiot." He opened his eyes and smiled. "Thanks, Lo."

Lo shook her head. "Let's just go."

She started toward the pier. Noah ran ahead. Lo tried to catch up, but considering his long legs and varsity training, she knew it was impossible. He already had the *Minke*'s engine sputtering by the time she clambered, gasping, into the passenger seat.

They sped across Gosport Harbor. The wind hit her face hard and cold. Every time they crossed a wave, the boat bounced high enough to lift her off her seat.

The engine moaned and coughed, but Noah pushed the throttle farther. Lo wanted to tell him it would stall, but she didn't think he'd be able to hear her, he was so focused and angry and terrified. Somehow they made it to White before the engine died.

"Tie her off, will you?" Noah said. He pulled off his dress shirt and jumped, still in his pants and white tee, into the black water. He swam a few lengths until his feet found bottom, and he ran the rest of the way, plunging through the shallows, his clothes wrapped dripping around him.

Lo waited for him to wade ashore before she took the wheel. She wasn't sure how well she could steer in the dark, but it was easier than she thought. She felt a growing bubble of pride in her chest as she guided the *Minke* safely to the dock and made it fast.

She jumped onto the beach and ran to the house, her chest still heaving from her first dash to the boat.

Inside, Gemm paced the kitchen floor. She heard Noah cursing in their bedroom upstairs.

"Are you okay, Gemm? Do you know what happened?"

Her grandmother shook her head and wrapped her green bathrobe tighter around her waist. Lo knew that bathrobe—she'd seen Maebh wearing it on her first morning here. Even in the midst of all this confusion, seeing it again made her smile.

"I was asleep," Gemm said, "and then it was as if I'd had a nightmare. I screamed and sat right up in bed, and my heart was just pounding away. I tried to remember the dream, but nothing came. It was as if I'd heard Maebh calling to me, and I couldn't reach her."

She pulled Lo into a hug and stroked her hair, as if the granddaughter, not the grandmother, needed comforting. "I'd only felt that once before, years ago. It was what made me leave your grandfather—well, that was part of it—and come back home to White. And tonight I felt it again, but Maebh hasn't come to me, and I don't know what to do. And now Noah's here, and he's in a panic about Mara . . . and I can't help but think that everything is just coming apart."

"Don't worry, Gemm," Lo said, wishing she could tell herself the same thing. "I'm sure one of them will come and explain soon."

She led her grandmother to the couch and sat her down. She put the kettle on the stove. Gemm was fond of saying that hot tea helped with any kind of crisis, and Lo thought they could both use some right now.

Noah crashed out of the bedroom and down the stairs. "Where is it? Damn it, where's her skin?"

"Her what?" Gemm's voice was startled, even horrified. "Noah—what on earth do you want with Mara's sealskin?"

"No, I—" He stopped, glancing around the room. He ran his hands frantically through his hair. "It's not like that, Gemm. I'm trying to find her. She's looking for her skin. If I look for it too—" He shook his head, his chest heaving. "Lo, you were with her when she got dressed. You have to know."

"Noah." Lo wished she knew how to calm him down. "She came ashore on this island, so it has to be somewhere. But I have no idea where she left it."

He stared past her, his eyes empty. He turned and rushed to the bathroom, letting its door slam behind him. Lo heard the crash of a medicine cabinet's worth of toiletries hitting the floor.

"Come on, Noah," she called. "She didn't leave it in the freaking bathroom." She was getting mad again. He'd dragged her away from Star just so she could stand around while he trashed the cottage? She imagined what their bedroom must look like: clothes and sheets tossed everywhere, drawers pulled out of the bureaus. "Noah, stop it! Just stop. You can't help her, okay?"

Noah emerged, his chest heaving, his shirt damp with seawater and sweat. "I have to," he said. "Maybe I'm being stupid, but I can't just— If you'd seen her face, Lo. I have to do something."

"I know." Lo looked out the window. "Maybe . . . Do you think she might have left it outside?" She pointed toward the lighthouse, but Noah was already at the door, outside before she'd even finished her sentence.

A gush of harsh wind pushed its way inside. Lo shivered. She moved to close the door, but she couldn't help watching as Noah ran toward the cliffs. She pictured him slipping down them, breaking a bone on the rocks and flailing in the sea with no one to save him—and then she knew she couldn't wait inside while he searched for the skin.

"I'm going to help him, Gemm," she said. She rushed after her brother. The kettle screeched behind her.

She reached the cliffs in time to watch Noah scramble down the last bit of near-vertical rock into the sharp, crashing waves at the bottom. There was a sudden drop into deep water not far from where he stood, and Lo shouted at him to remember it.

Noah looked up at Lo and nodded. He seemed to yell

something back to her, but the waves crashed against the cliffs and Lo couldn't hear him.

She saw a shape in the water, heading in from the open ocean and straight toward Noah. It was dark and slick, and at first Lo thought it was a shark. Then it found footing and rose out of the water.

Mara stalked toward Noah, her body draped with something dirty and wet that must once have been Lo's dress. Even from the top of the cliffs, Lo could see the livid anger on her face.

Mara sprang through the water and tackled Noah, battering him against the rocks. Lo screamed, too far away to help.

twenty-eight

SINKING

NOAH choked on the seawater and spit that rammed into his windpipe. Mara slammed him against the cliff again. She was saying something, but he could barely hear. He coughed and pushed back at her.

Her eyes widened, her mouth opened, and she backed away from him into deeper water. She began to shiver. Lo's pearl headband hung from her hair like a broken crown.

"You don't have it."

"No."

She shuddered. "Thank the Goddess." She looked up at him, her eyes moving over his arms and chest.

Noah stayed still, splayed against the rocks. He didn't want to move until he could be sure she wouldn't tackle him again. For someone at least six inches shorter than he was, she'd hit him with incredible — inhuman — force.

She moved forward slowly, but Noah could tell she was ready to strike again if she needed to. The problem was, he still didn't know what had provoked her in the first place. *Yes*, he thought, *staying still is definitely my best option.*

"Mara," he said, slowly and carefully, "please tell me what's happened. I thought—" He pushed away the memory of what he'd felt when they kissed. "I thought we understood each other, but then you ran off like that, and I didn't know if you were hurt or . . . Please, just tell me."

She growled and reached toward him, stopping just before her hand connected with his throat. "As if you don't know."

"What? I—"

"Stop." Her voice was cold, harsh, and he could hear it starting to break. He saw water speckling her face, but he didn't know whether it was tears or spray.

"Just stop pretending, Noah. I know what you did. I know why you're looking for it." She sucked in air through her teeth. "I'm only grateful you haven't found it yet." She stalked past him to a dark, hidden hole in the cliffs, plunged her hand into it, and retrieved her damp, shining skin.

He peeled himself away from the rocks and took a cautious step toward her, the girl he'd held in his arms less than two hours ago.

She spun and glared at him. He didn't need the warning that rocketed through their new connection to know he had to back off.

She took a few steps toward him, moving onto higher ground. She looked down and met his eyes.

Even then, knowing she hated him, he thought she was beautiful. He'd never seen anyone so fierce.

"Do you see this?" she asked, clutching her sealskin. "It will never be yours, never."

"Mara, I don't want—"

"Shut up," she rasped. "Just listen. You have him now; your friends at the Center have him, but we will find a way to get him back. And if you hurt him . . . If you hurt him, I will kill you." She smiled, her lips drawn, her teeth white and glistening.

"Mara—"

But she vanished into the water. Only a ripple was left behind her to mark where she'd stood.

Noah stared out at the ocean. He could still feel an echo of her pain in his chest, but his own drowned it out. He thought he was starting to understand what had happened.

Mara thought he had taken her skin, like the fisherman in Gemm's story. He hated that she thought he could do such a thing. And the "him" she'd spoken of—God, that must be another kidnapped youngling.

Noah's stomach twisted with guilt, and his vision blurred. He steadied himself on a jutting rock.

I wanted to find her, so I looked for her skin—but as it turned out, that was exactly the worst thing he could have done. Noah felt along the rock face, searching for a way back up. There was nothing. He didn't know how he'd gotten down the cliff without breaking his neck.

He'd have to swim around to the beach. He turned back

toward the ocean, preparing to dive, and saw a glimmer in the water.

He swam to it in a few quick, broad strokes. He knew —he told himself—it wasn't Mara, but he couldn't keep from hoping that she'd realized he was innocent. Maybe she'd come back to forgive him.

His hands found the source of the glimmer, but his eyes were still bleary with salt. Noah groped at it, a soft slither in his hands like an eel. For a horrible moment he thought it might be another lost sealskin.

Then he recognized the feel of Mara's dress from when they'd danced, when he'd held her. Noah opened his raw eyes and saw a ragged swath of green silk in his hands, destroyed by dirt and seawater.

Noah released it back into the ocean. Mara had discarded it, and he would too—it wasn't as if Lo would want it back now. He watched the dress slide over the water until a large wave clipped over it and pulled it down.

He dove again and swam to the beach. The power in his arms and legs surprised him. He knew he should have been exhausted long ago, but adrenaline sparked in his muscles and he couldn't help but swim quickly, his limbs pushing through the water with a manic energy.

Noah winced as his foot connected with a sharp underwater stone. He surfaced and clutched at the wound, squinting to see it in the moonlight. Threads of blood wove out between his fingers. He prodded his instep, and a long slice of skin flapped back at him.

He found his footing in the water and waded to shore. Limping toward the cottage, he focused on the light in the upstairs window. He knew Lo and Gemm were worried, but he couldn't bring himself to care. The salt water dripping into his wound sent a deep and throbbing pain up his shin, but he didn't care about that, either.

His mind was on Mara, somewhere out in the darkness, in the cold and wind and water. Noah knew he'd never been in as much pain as he'd seen on her face tonight.

He knew with equal certainty that whatever he'd done — whatever she thought he had done — she wouldn't ever forgive him.

twenty-nine

SEEK

L O tried to unclench her fists and loosen the knots in her back. She could see Noah wading onto the beach, only fifty feet away. She knew he was safe now — safer than he'd been before — but she couldn't make herself relax.

When Mara had attacked him like that, Lo had felt a hot surge of protective anger. She'd never felt so aggressive before, as if she could really hurt Mara if she got the chance. But in the same instant, Lo had known that her body was too weak to fight, or even to scramble down the cliffs the way Noah had. Her aggression had leaked away. In that moment, Lo had hated her body's weakness more than she'd ever hated its size. She'd felt ridiculous for ever thinking her body was *big.* She'd felt tiny and weak and helpless, watching her brother in danger and knowing she'd hurt herself so much that she couldn't help him.

Noah stumbled over the rocks. She ran toward him, promising herself she'd run again tomorrow, and the next day, and the next, until she was strong. She took his arm and draped it over her shoulder, trying to support him.

"Are you all right?"

Noah moved his head, but she couldn't tell if he meant yes or no. She braced her arm against his back. "Come on," she said. "You need to get inside."

Gemm waited for them, mugs of fresh tea steaming beside her. As soon as they walked in, she snatched the old knitted throw off the couch and wrapped it around them.

"Now, please," she said, "someone tell me what on earth is going on."

Noah and Lo looked at each other, silent. The anguish on Noah's face was too awful for Lo to see. She looked away.

And then she burst out laughing.

Gemm frowned. Noah, if possible, looked even worse than he had a moment ago.

"I'm sorry—I know it's—" Lo gasped, shaking so hard that the blanket slipped from her shoulders. She took a deep breath. She stopped laughing, but as soon as she quieted, tears started in her eyes. "I really am sorry." Another breath. "It's just . . ." She took yet another breath. "You know, a few weeks ago I wouldn't have believed any of it."

Noah managed a quiet chuckle. "I know."

Gemm tucked the blanket around Lo again and returned to the stove. "I'll believe it, if someone will just tell me what it is," she grumbled.

Noah laughed again, louder this time. "I'll tell you, Gemm," he said, standing up. "You can sit here, with Lo. I'll bring your tea over."

Gemm reached up and stroked his hair. "A good boy on both counts." She lowered herself onto the couch.

Lo leaned her head on her grandmother's shoulder. After the cold and dark and panic of the last few hours, it was good to feel so warm and safe. Her chest was still tight with suppressed tears or laughter — she could no longer tell which — but it didn't matter. They were back with Gemm, and Noah would explain, and somehow things would work out.

"Mara thinks I want to take her skin," Noah said. "The whole pod's panicking. I think one of their — their children was kidnapped."

Lo felt her grandmother flinch. But Gemm stayed silent, and Noah continued.

"I think it happened during the dance," he said. "Everything was fine — more than fine . . ." His face burned red.

Lo smiled to herself. She'd seen him and Mara dancing together. She remembered wishing that someday someone would look at her the way Noah looked at Mara. More than fine, indeed.

Noah raised his eyebrows at Lo, and she removed the knowing smirk from her face.

"Anyway," he said pointedly, "things were going pretty well, but then Mara just freaked out. She ran out of the tent, and I followed her, and we —" He stopped and blushed again.

"Yes?" asked Gemm.

"Well, then she panicked. She screamed, and she ran toward the rocks and started digging through them as if she'd forgotten her skin was back here . . ." He shook his head. "I don't know. It was bad. And then she dove into the water and swam away, and it was so dark—I had no idea where she'd gone."

Noah collapsed onto one of the dining chairs, its legs creaking under his weight. He raked his hands through his hair—the sun had bleached it almost white by now—and sighed deeply before speaking again.

"I didn't know what I could do, but I had to do something. I had to try to find her. I thought if I could find her skin, I'd find her, too. I don't know.

"Only I guess something happened out . . . wherever she was . . . that made her think I was helping whoever took her brother. She thinks someone from the Center took him. And when she did come back here, she found me in the water, and I guess she thought—" His voice broke. "She thought I wanted to take her skin, too."

He looked up, his face drawn, red lines spidering in his eyes. "God, Gemm, I'm such an idiot. I couldn't—I can't —help her, and she'll always hate me now."

"Oh, honey." Gemm walked over to hug Noah. "That's not true. You tried to do the right thing. I'll talk to Maebh, tell her what happened. I'm sure it will work out."

Lo heard a tremor in Gemm's voice, and she wondered if her grandmother believed what she was saying.

Gemm stood up, staring out the window at the black ocean. Lo couldn't tell what she was looking for.

"I'll stay up and wait for Maebh," Gemm said. "I know she'll want to see me." Her wrinkled face creased deeper with worry, but she smiled at her grandchildren. "You should both go to bed. I can't imagine how tired you must be."

It was as if Gemm's words broke through a wall of adrenaline Lo had built up inside her body. She yawned, wincing at the ache in her legs and spine.

She looked at Noah, and he nodded. They trudged up the stairs.

The room was in shambles: drawers pulled all the way out of both dressers, clothes everywhere, Lo's empty suitcases dragged from under her bed. For once in her life, she was too tired to care about the mess. As soon as Noah disappeared behind the folding screen that divided their bedroom, Lo changed into her pajamas. She pulled back her sheets and buried herself in the cool softness of her bed.

The window creaked open.

"Just leave it," she mumbled. "Go to sleep."

"Not happening," said Noah.

Lo slowly pushed herself out of bed and walked to his side of the screen. "What d'you mean?" She yawned hugely and felt a pop in the back of her jaw. She groaned and rubbed her cheek.

"I'm going back to the Center," he said. "I want to see if I can find out anything to help Mara—to help the pod. Or at least—maybe it's not anyone from the Center at all, and I can prove it. You can come, if you want, but be quiet about it if you're staying. I don't want Gemm to worry."

Lo glanced back at her bed. The sheets were crumpled into a soft nest, probably still warm from her body. All she wanted was to settle into that nest and sleep, maybe for days.

She looked at Noah. Dark half-moons spread under his eyes, and his hands were clenched into white-knuckled fists.

"Okay," she said. "I'll go with you." She yawned again. "But you definitely owe me one for this."

Noah rolled his eyes. "Great," he said. "Let's get going."

thirty

CHASE

NOAH imagined them tying sheets together and climbing out the window, like they do in old prison-escape movies. He got as far as pulling all the sheets off his bed before he realized there was no place to tie them.

His head throbbing, he sank to the floor in despair, too tired to think quickly. It was Lo, in the end, who figured out how they would manage their escape.

"You go first," she said. "I think I can hold you if you climb quickly. Then I'll go downstairs and talk Gemm into going to bed. I'm in my pajamas already, so she won't think anything of it. We shouldn't get her involved in any more of this—God knows she's been through enough tonight. I'll at least get her to go in her room and rest a bit, and then I'll meet you outside." She frowned. "I think we'll have to take the rowboat, since she would hear the *Minke*'s engine."

Noah nodded. "Okay. I'll row, but you have to be lookout, since it's dark and I'll be facing backwards."

Lo looked so confident laying out her plan, her head high, her back straight. He hadn't seen her stand like that in so long — usually she slouched and hunched her shoulders, as if she were trying to vanish inside herself. He tried not to make too much of the change, but it sent a pulse of hope through him.

He smiled at her. He needed hope just then, even if it came in the form of his little sister in her ridiculous crossword-puzzle-print pajamas.

He finished tying the sheets together and fed them out the window. They vanished like an eel into the darkness.

"Lean against the wall," he told Lo. "You can put a foot under the window, like this, and let it take a lot of the weight."

She nodded. "Got it." She picked up the end of the last sheet, and Noah tried not to think about how weak her arms looked. He just had to believe she would be able to hold him.

He climbed out and gripped the sheet in one hand, clinging to the windowsill with the other. He braced his feet against outside the wall and, holding his breath, he let go of the window.

The sheets pulled tight and groaned as the knots adjusted. He heard Lo breathe in. He looked up.

"Just go," she hissed through clenched teeth. "Christ, you're heavy."

Noah stared at her in surprise. She smiled at him, and they both had to laugh.

He wrapped his legs around the rope and slid down. Then he crept over the island to the *Gull*. He realized he hadn't pulled it past the tide line the last time he'd used it; the edge of the water lapped the boat's stern, pulling it toward the sea one wave at a time. Another half hour and it would have floated away.

Noah pictured the boat drifting all the way out into the open Atlantic, a tiny red dot on an unfathomably huge expanse of water. A prayer his mother had taught him as a child floated in on his memory: *For thy ocean is so big, and my boat is so small. Amen.* He couldn't remember the beginning of the prayer, but he figured the ending must have been the important part.

He took the oars from the long metal trunk on the shore. When he came back to the boat, Lo was waiting for him, still in her pajamas. She'd rolled up the pants to her knees and waded into the surf, pulling the boat after her.

"You didn't even put on your shoes?" he asked.

Lo shook her head. "Doesn't matter, no time. Let's go." She glanced back toward the island, her eyes flickering with sadness.

"Is it Gemm?" Noah asked, holding the boat steady while Lo climbed in.

Lo swiped her fingers over her cheeks. "Yeah. She's just miserable. She was crying when I came downstairs, and she tried to hide it, but that just made everything worse, you know? She loves Maebh more than anything, I mean, anyone could tell that, but Maebh hasn't come to her and she can't do anything to help. She's so afraid."

He sighed and climbed into the boat after her. "I'm sure she'll come soon," he said, to himself as well as to Lo. Maebh loved Gemm, really loved her, even though Gemm had once hurt her so much, if the story Lo had told him was true. Maebh would come to her. He had to believe that if Maebh still loved Gemm, he could win Mara back too. He could show her he was innocent.

He remembered her under the cliff shadows, her face panicked, the shreds of her dress tossed in the waves. She'd wanted to kill him, and he'd still wanted to help her. He could still feel the pulse of her emotions — what she'd called their link — and all he wanted was to soothe her pain.

Noah took a deep breath and kept rowing toward the Center. If he couldn't help her, was he just risking his job for nothing? Was he throwing away his whole future?

But that didn't matter, either. Even if she would always hate him — and sensing the echo of their link in his body, he thought maybe she would — he had to do this. Even if it was useless, stupid — he had to try.

"A bit to port," Lo said. "There's a bunch of lobster traps just there."

Noah nodded and pulled them away.

They were almost at the pier, but the harbor felt larger

and darker to Noah than it ever had before. Waves rocked the rowboat, spattering cold water onto their legs.

He felt suddenly as if he'd spent the whole summer out here, between the islands, tossed on the waves. He could barely recall the feeling of standing on solid ground.

"About here," Lo said. "Slow down."

Noah craned his head around and saw the pier looming toward them. He swept up an oar and braced it against the wood, pulling them in.

The boat's hull bumped against a piling. Noah climbed onto the pier and reached for the rope.

Lo pushed his hands away. "I'll tie her off," she said. "You get to the Center and start looking."

Noah nodded. "Thanks." Between the rocky ground and the darkness, he couldn't run as fast as usual, even under the full moon. Every step set off a shock of pain from the cut on his foot.

As he rounded a corner and approached the Center's entrance, Noah remembered he didn't have a key. He stopped and stared at the door, trying to remember how thick it was.

He backed up a few paces and rushed forward, slamming his shoulder against it. The impact was louder than he expected. It sent a clanging echo into the night—and, he was sure, into every room of the Center. Anyone inside would know he was there.

His shoulder throbbed. He prodded it carefully and winced. He took stock of all the injuries he'd accrued in the last few hours: this new bruise, the slice down his instep, and the marks on his neck where Mara had briefly throttled him. *Why am I helping her, again?*

But then he imagined how he'd feel if he thought Mara had tried to hurt Lo. He knew he couldn't blame Mara for anything she'd done that night. He could only blame himself for not doing more to help her.

At least that part he could try to fix. Noah backed up again, preparing to ram his aching shoulder against the door one more time.

"Stop!" Lo cried as he took his first lunging step.

He skidded forward, grasping for balance as his feet slid over dew-slicked pebbles. He looked back at his sister. "What is it?" he hissed. "And not so loud, Lo, Christ."

Lo rolled her eyes. She lifted a hand to her hair and pulled out one of the pins that held back her bangs. "You seriously never learned how to do this?" she asked, pushing him away from the door frame. She squinted at the lock and stuck her pin inside.

"You seriously did? I guess I should give you more credit."

"Well, obviously." Lo smirked, still squinting at the lock. "And it's not as though you have bobby pins, I guess." She sighed with satisfaction as the door swung open. "It's weird Professor Foster didn't give you a key, though, since you're always yammering on about being his protégé."

Noah nodded absently. "Only he has the keys to this place. The older interns say he's kind of neurotic about it. And he has that giant key chain   "

He frowned. He'd seen Professor Foster's key chain so many times. Besides the keys it held, there hadn't been much to it: no grocery store discount cards or ID tags or anything decorative—except for one small circle of gray leather. It was a kind of leather he knew well now.

"Lo," he said carefully, "do you remember what Professor Foster's key chain looks like?"

"What? I guess so." She quirked her eyebrows at him, then frowned, trying to remember. "Why does it matter? It's not as if it's around, and anyway it was just a big tangle of keys and—" Her breath hitched. "And an old bit of leather. Of—of sealskin. Noah, do you think—"

"Yes." Noah pushed his hands through his hair, trying to think over his audibly pounding heart. The logical part of his mind pushed in at him, reminding him that just because Professor Foster had sealskin on his key chain didn't mean he was a kidnapper. But the professor's secrecy, the strange sounds in his house, that gut feeling of *wrong* Noah had felt all through dinner . . . It had to be him.

The first steps of a plan were forming in his exhausted mind, and he didn't have time to wait for the rest of it. He would do the only thing he had left: He would help. He would try.

"We have to go to Professor Foster's house," he said. "Now."

"What? We have to look for the skins. They could be here. We have to check the labs, Professor Foster's office . . . even the filing room. God knows what's in those boxes." She laughed a little.

He looked down the island to their tiny rowboat's mooring. "I don't want to leave you."

But he remembered how Professor Foster had treated his dog. If that really was a child, Mara's sister . . . he had to go, had to stop him, right now. And when he brought the children back, they'd need their skins, or they wouldn't be free. He knew Lo was right.

He looked at his sister. "Even if you do find something, how will you get back?"

Lo pointed toward the pier. "The Center has, like, four boats. The keys are in Professor Foster's office, and I can definitely get in there." She waved the bobby pin at him. "I'll be fine. Noah, please. You said I could help."

He shook his head. "I just don't want you to get hurt."

"I know." She stepped forward and hugged him. "You either. But we have to help them. Like you said."

He looked toward White, where the lighthouse beam flashed and the kitchen window glowed a steady yellow speck. "You have to tell Gemm what's happened," he said.

"You have to get Maebh and Mara to believe that I—that we didn't do this. That it's Professor Foster."

"I know." Lo let go of him and turned to go inside.

Noah didn't want to think about what would happen if he was wrong. He'd lose his internship, of course, and his college scholarship—he'd probably end up in jail.

He took a deep breath and walked to the pier. He jumped into the *Gull*, raising waves around him that crashed a thin layer of seawater into the boat. It soaked through his shoes, freezing his skin and stinging the long cut on his foot.

Noah took in the ropes and shoved off, pulling at the oars with what remained of his strength. All he had to do was get to White, he told his shaking muscles. Once he had the motorboat, everything would be fine.

Over his shoulder, he watched Gemm's cottage grow larger as he approached. His bruised shoulder was growing stiff, and he groaned to distract himself from the pain.

A dark figure stood on the crest of the island. His heart pounded and he hoped for Mara, but then the lighthouse illuminated gray hair and Gemm's worried face.

He thought he still might get away without her noticing—he didn't want to put her through anything else tonight. But she turned toward him, squinting through the darkness.

"Who's there?" she called, stepping warily toward the shore.

"Gemm, it's me." His voice cracked, and his breaths rattled from his dry throat.

She ran toward him, into the waves. She grasped the bow of the *Gull*, and he climbed out so they could bring it ashore together. "Noah! Where have you been?"

"The Center." They pulled the boat far up from the tide line.

Noah stared at his grandmother, wondering how to make her understand what he had to do.

"I have to take—I mean, I'd like to take the *Minke* out, Gemm, please." He knew he sounded like a little boy learning his manners—except for the shaky desperation in his voice.

Gemm frowned. "Why?"

Noah exhaled. "I'm trying to help them. Please, I don't have time to explain. Just let me take the boat. Gemm, please."

She nodded. "Of course you can take her if you need to. But, goodness, Noah, I wish someone would let me help too. Maebh—" Her hand darted to her mouth, as if to stifle a sob Noah couldn't hear. "Maebh still hasn't come to me."

Noah didn't know what to say to that. He waded toward the *Minke*, moored at the end of Gemm's dock. The tide was at its lowest, so he could walk all the way out to the boat and lift himself aboard. His spent limbs protested the effort, but Noah ignored them.

Gemm made a guttural sound in her throat, a groan or a

chuckle. "I suppose it was foolish of me to think you'd stay in your bed when I told you to." She sighed.

"I guess so." Noah tried to smile at her, to reassure her. "Don't worry, Gemm. I just have to do this."

"I know." Gemm touched her face again, but she no longer looked on the verge of tears. A sad distance swept over her eyes. "I was young and in love once too."

He turned the key in the ignition. As the engine sputtered to life, he pushed away the thought that Gemm might know more about his feelings for Mara than he did himself. He would sort that out later. All he knew now was that he had to help her.

The *Minke* sped out toward the mainland, water churning a thick white trail in her wake.

thirty-one

SKIN

MARA refused. There was nothing Maebh could say to make her leave the younglings ever, ever again—let alone to make her go back to White. She didn't want to set foot or flipper anywhere near Noah.

Maebh sat next to her on Whale Rock, her sealskin half shed, trying to reason with her, but Mara wasn't interested in any reasoning besides her own. She kept her skin on and glared at the Elder through seal eyes.

"Listen to me, Mara," Maebh said. Branna and Tavis were piled over each other on her lap, and she stroked them absentmindedly with her human hands. The others were circling the harbor with Ronan. He was teaching them to hunt minnows, trying to distract them from Lir's absence.

Nothing could distract Mara. She'd been stupid, lethally stupid, and Noah had betrayed her. All she wanted was to sit with that knowledge, to feel the guilt entering her body like a knife. She didn't want Maebh's comfort. She didn't deserve it.

She turned from the Elder, staring into the black,

choppy water. She felt a hand touch her flipper, and she jerked it away.

Her sealskin pulled back, sliding off her forearm. Mara stared at the still-raw splits in her webbed fingers. She felt her skin parting, slipping from her shoulders and onto the rock, until she was human down to her thighs.

"Goddess!" she swore, yanking off the rest of her skin. She didn't know why her own body kept disobeying her like this.

At least now, with human speech in her mouth, she could tell Maebh to leave her alone. But the expression on the Elder's face, so loving and worried, made her hesitate. She gathered up her sealskin and hugged it, leaning her chest into its warmth. She felt her ribs shake as she cried.

When Maebh touched her back, she could not bring herself to flinch away again.

"You're wondering why this is happening to you," Maebh said, "and why you cannot keep your form. I think I know."

Mara rubbed her face dry and looked up at Maebh. "You do?"

The Elder nodded. "I am linked with Dolores," she said, her voice low and sad. "I sometimes wish it weren't so, but I cannot change it. As soon as I loved her, we were linked. Even when we'd been apart for years, when I told myself every day how much I hated her . . . I stayed a seal for forty years, unable to look at my own humanskin without aching for hers. I never aged, never grew, because of her. But the link was there. I couldn't dissolve it, couldn't burn it away with anger, much as I wanted to. Much as I wanted not to love her. My body wouldn't let me change, and yours isn't letting you stay a seal—but it's all the same. I know. I know how frightening it is."

Maebh's hand drifted up and down Mara's back to the rhythm of her own slow breath.

Mara inhaled, her chest shuddering. New air rushed into her lungs.

"Once you love someone, part of you is bound forever. Perhaps you never see him again—perhaps your life is better without him, and it's right to be apart. But once you've loved him, the link is formed. You can ignore it if you choose, but you cannot sever it."

"I can." Mara shoved her feet into her sealskin and willed her two halves to meld together.

Nothing happened.

"Christ!" She pulled her sealskin off and tossed it toward Maebh. "Why is this happening? Why can't I just be a seal?"

Maebh's fingers brushed over Mara's sealskin. "Why do you think it is, Daughter?"

"I don't know!" Mara tugged her hands through her hair, working through the stubborn spikes that always appeared after a quick change.

"Mm." Maebh watched the White Island lighthouse

sweep its beam across the harbor. "You swore like a human just then—did you notice?"

"I—" Mara pulled her fingers away from her head. She remembered how Noah ran his hands through his hair, just like that. Had she learned anything else from him, without meaning to? "I guess I did." She looked at Maebh, waiting for an explanation.

The Elder nodded, looking in her eyes as if she expected Mara to realize something.

Mara returned her stare, waiting.

"I think there is a part of you," Maebh said, "that wants to be human. That is why you're rejecting your skin. You don't truly want it, and I imagine it's been a while since you have. I think this has happened to you before." She smiled gently. "Am I wrong?"

Mara crossed her arms over her breasts, suddenly chilled in the night air. "You're wrong, Maebh. I hate this body. All it's done is confuse me, ever since my first change, and now . . . and now it's cost us Lir."

She let that unfurl across the space between her and Maebh, out into the water and up to the sky. She didn't think there was enough depth in the ocean to contain her guilt, her hatred for her human body and the way it had betrayed her secrets into Noah's confidence. Betrayed Lir into his keeping.

"No, Mara." Maebh stroked her back again. "Lir's loss is not your fault. You were not at the ceremony. I was there.

Ronan was. If anyone is to bear the burden of this guilt, it is we. It is I. I knew it was dangerous, and still I allowed it."

Mara shifted and leaned her head on Maebh's shoulder. She thought they might collapse under the combined weight of their grief, but Maebh was like a pillar, holding her up. Shared, the pain was doubled, but only half so crippling. Mara couldn't bring herself to wish for the strength to stand alone.

"We have to go back to White," said Maebh.

Mara felt the pillar collapse. She jerked her head off Maebh's shoulder. "No." She scrambled away, to the very edge of Whale Rock. "I'm never going back there again."

"Mara." Maebh reached toward her, pleading. "Think of Dolores. We're linked. She knows I'm afraid, but she doesn't know why. Even if you're right about Noah—and I believe you, of course I do," she added quickly, "I can't make myself believe that Dolores would hurt the pod like this."

She spoke confidently, but Mara thought she felt a shadow of doubt cross over their link. "Please, Mara, come with me. You shouldn't lose your faith in humans, simply because some have wronged us so." She smoothed her hands over her sealskin. "Besides," she said, "Dolores is Noah's grandmother, after all. Perhaps she'll be able to help us find Lir."

Lir and Aine, Mara's mind whispered. Her sister's name

rose in her throat, but she couldn't say it. She pressed her lips together.

Three dark heads appeared in the harbor and started toward them — Ronan and the younglings.

"Tavis, Branna," Maebh said, stroking the fine fur on the younglings' heads, "I need you to stay with your brother for a little while."

They crawled out of Maebh's lap and into the water. Mara watched them until they reached their siblings.

Ronan nodded at them, his eyes guarded and sharp. They disappeared under the water.

"All right," Maebh said. "It's time to go."

Mara had to try one more time. "Surely you won't leave the younglings alone again so soon?"

Maebh shook her head. "You underestimate your brother, Mara," she said. "He is strong, and he bears the weight of his own guilt tonight. He will not let them be harmed." A subtle look crossed her face, as if she'd just thought of some clever secret. "Besides," she added, "an Elder must know how to divide responsibility. It's a lesson you will do well to learn."

Mara frowned. It sounded as if Maebh were giving advice to an heir, a future Elder. Mara thought she'd never be ready, after Aine was lost, and now Lir . . . Mara had buried her hope of becoming the Elder, of restoring the pod, in the deepest part of her soul, far away from where she kept her dreams.

But now Maebh was pulling that hope to the surface again. Mara wanted to be the Elder much more than she wanted to stay away from Noah; Maebh knew that.

So when the Elder plunged into the water and started swimming toward White, Mara followed. She knew she didn't have a choice.

thirty-two

FOUND

NOAH held his breath. He knew he had to be absolutely quiet.

Quiet hadn't been easy, not in this house. Noah was thankful that at least the den window had been cracked open, or he didn't know how he would have gotten in without making noise. But Professor Foster's staircase creaked even worse than Gemm's, and the pain that still throbbed in his foot made it hard to tread softly.

He'd made it to the top of the stairs, at least. There were three doors in the upstairs hall, and Noah stopped, unsure which to try. It was dark, and the strongest impression he got was the smell, something that made him think of expired cleaning solutions—at once too clean and not clean enough. Something chemical.

He heard Professor Foster behind the farthest door.

"It's okay," the professor murmured. He sounded genuinely concerned. "You're okay."

Noah walked slowly down the hall. Was it possible,

233

even now, that Professor Foster was innocent? That he had a dog, after all?

The door was slightly open. He kept still. He hoped, he wished, that he'd been wrong.

"See? It's over now." Professor Foster spoke quietly, gently. "I told you it wouldn't hurt much."

He looked down and saw two sliding bolt locks on the outside of the door. They were both undone.

"All right. Stay. I'll be back soon."

It took Noah a moment to understand—Professor Foster was coming out. If he found him like this, hiding in the hallway . . . Noah couldn't let that happen. He glanced around for a place to hide. He didn't know if he could get to one of the other doors before the professor emerged, and anyway, they might be locked.

It was still possible that he was innocent. That Noah had misjudged him, this man he admired so much.

He wrapped his hand around the edge of the door and pushed it open.

"I'm sorry—" he started to say.

Another hand gripped his and wrenched him inside.

He felt an arm wrap hard around his neck, and before he had time to register anything else, a sharp slip of pain under his shoulder blade, something invading, something cold. And something else, hot and wet, sliding down his back.

He shuddered. His knees unlocked under him and he fell.

"You . . ." He tried to speak again, but oh, his shoulder didn't like that. He hissed his breath back in.

Professor Foster knelt beside him, a knife slicked bloody in his hand. "Noah?" he asked. "You—why in God's name did you come here?"

Noah pushed himself up. His vision fogged and then cleared.

Two children huddled together in the far corner of the room, two pale children with black hair and wide black eyes, wearing old, worn white T-shirts too big for them. They looked almost identical. One, though, was scarred— scarred everywhere, in an angled grid over her face and neck and arms. Old scars.

Aine.

Noah pulled away from Professor Foster. Slowly, every muscle crying out with the effort, he stood. His legs trembled, and he felt the blood pulse faster from the wound in his back. He knew he wouldn't be able to stand for long.

But Professor Foster didn't have to know that. "You can't do this," he said. "I came to—" His ribs convulsed under a fresh wave of pain. He leaned back against the wall behind him, trying to stand as if he didn't need the support. "You have to give them back to their family. They're just—they're just kids." He looked over at Aine's grid of scars, at the way the children clung to each other and stared. "I know you hurt them."

Professor Foster closed his eyes. He nodded, slowly, heavily. He stayed silent for a long time, and Noah waited, just praying he could stay standing.

"I know it seems that way," the professor said. "I know what this must look like to you. And I'm sorry. I am. But think about this, Noah." His eyes darted around the room, not focusing on anything there—it seemed he was imagining some other place, somewhere far away. "You've read my work on sealskin. This is a whole other level. I've done amazing things with selkie skin already—I've had Hope's skin for years now. Just ingesting it makes me feel—it's incredible. They—I—*we* could save the Center with this. My God, we could save lives."

His voice had grown quick and manic as he spoke. He'd been inching closer to Noah, and now he laid a hand on his shoulder, then slid it around his neck.

"I'm sorry," he said again, and his grip tightened, and he slammed Noah's head backwards.

Noah felt a crack and dropped to the floor, black rushing over his eyes.

thirty-three

TRUTH

THE cottage looked the same as it had earlier that evening, shabby and comfortable, warm light pouring from the windows. The crooked path to the front door reminded Mara of Noah holding her hand as they walked in together, the day she'd told him the truth. His fingers had been gentle against hers, his sweatshirt soft on her skin. The door creaked, and she remembered how he'd opened it for her on the very first day they'd met.

Inside was worse. The pink couch, the worn kitchen table, the old whitewashed walls — they felt so familiar, as if Mara had been coming here her whole life. As if she belonged here. She'd thought the walls would be darker, the photos hung on them more sinister, but everything was as cramped and cluttered and wonderful as it had been before.

She closed her eyes, unable to bear how she still loved this house and treasured her memories of it. She hated herself for feeling this way.

When she opened her eyes again, Maebh and Noah's grandmother were sitting together on the couch. Maebh wrapped her arm around Gemm, as if the human were the one in mourning.

Mara's lip curled back in an almost-snarl. No relative of Noah's had a right to Maebh's comfort, not now.

"I didn't know; I didn't know," Gemm whispered in an empty voice that nearly softened Mara's anger.

Then she saw Noah's sweatshirt slung over one of the kitchen chairs, and she hardened again.

"I know you didn't," Maebh said, twirling a length of Gemm's gray hair in her fingers. "I'm so sorry."

Mara scoffed. She stalked to the bathroom door, the farthest she could get from Maebh and her disgusting human romance. It was all weakness, and stupidity, and loss. Mara's humanskin prickled with anger, and she hated the feeling of it.

"I'm sorry I didn't come earlier," Maebh said. "We didn't know what had happened, at first, and I needed to keep the other younglings safe. I know you must have felt it; you must have wondered." She pressed her lips to Gemm's cheek.

Mara's heart cramped and ached, but she didn't look away again. Instead, she sent Maebh all her impatience, all her fear about where Lir could be, what he could be enduring.

Maebh turned to Mara, her eyes hard. "Yes, Daughter," she said. "I know your fears. Patience becomes an Elder too."

The dream grew in her again, and an image appeared clear as water in her mind. She saw the younglings changing, Ronan free and searching for other pods, and Mara herself leading all of them, helping them, letting the pod evolve and change as it should always have done. When Maebh offered the dream to her like that, Mara knew she'd do whatever she could for the chance to reach out and claim it.

She would even stay human. She would even listen to Gemm try to defend Noah, pointless as she knew that would be. She grudgingly walked back toward the couch and perched herself on its arm. She crossed her legs, folded her hands together, and attempted to radiate patience.

Maebh chuckled. "Thank you, Mara."

Gemm lifted her head, wiping away the tears that had settled into the wrinkles around her eyes. "I don't expect either of you to trust me," she said.

"Oh—" Maebh started, but Gemm hushed her with a look.

"I've betrayed you before, love. I know it was years ago, but I don't deserve your trust. I know that. All I can do now is tell you the truth, and hope that somehow you will believe me." She glanced up at Mara.

Mara nodded slowly. She tried to look patient and encouraging; she tried to make sure those were the only emotions Maebh could sense through their link.

"I understand why you think Noah is involved," Gemm said, "but I promise he's not."

Mara couldn't hold her growl in this time. It ripped from her throat like a clawed animal, low and fierce. "You're wrong," she hissed, her human voice sounding animal too.

"No," said Maebh, shaking her head gently, "she's not."

Mara almost stormed out to the ocean then. Only the call of the dream, the hope that Maebh might make her the Elder soon, held her back.

She tried to ignore her other reason for staying: the bright and throbbing and all-too-human part of her that wished Gemm were telling the truth about the boy she'd kissed.

"All right," she said. "I'll listen."

Gemm settled closer to Maebh. "I saw Noah tonight, after the dance. He was scared—terrified—that you were hurt, Mara. He didn't know what was going on. He didn't understand anything. All he wanted was to help you. He was looking for your skin"—Mara bristled—"because he was looking for *you*. After you came, and he realized what you thought of him, he was so miserable and exhausted that I told him to go to sleep, and still he snuck out and rowed to the Center to see if he could find the kidnapper there. I suppose he found something, because he came back here half an hour ago and—and he took my boat to the mainland." Tears shimmered in her eyes again. "He didn't tell me where he was going, but I know well enough it's somewhere dangerous, and he's doing it for you."

Mara shook her head. "No. No, he's not."

"Mara." Maebh's voice was kind but firm. "I know you linked with Noah tonight. I could feel it — the whole pod could feel it, for Goddess's sake."

Mara's face burned, but Maebh and Gemm only smiled at each other, sharing some secret memory.

"Search that link, child, and tell me if Noah means you harm."

Almost against her will, a curious tendril crept up in Mara, searching out Noah's emotions. She sensed nothing, at first. Then came confusion, disorientation, fear.

She frowned — *Is he hurt?* — then chided herself for caring if he was. Nevertheless, she could find nothing dishonest or cruel in his feelings toward her. She recognized heat and longing in him, and she trembled as those same feelings leapt up in her.

She hardly trusted herself to speak, with her heat twining through Noah's in their link. She shook her head.

"Good," said the Elder. She looked at Gemm again. "Now, did Noah tell you anything else about who might have . . . taken Lir?"

Gemm exhaled. "No. He didn't tell me anything." She raised her eyebrows, and a tiny flash of hope warmed her face. "But Lo's still upstairs," she said. "Maybe he told her."

The door to Noah and Lo's room was closed. Gemm opened it quietly, so as not to surprise Lo while she slept.

Her bed was disheveled, the white sheets twisted into

peaks like foaming waves. Mara could see part of Noah's bed beyond a folding screen. She stepped forward, curious to see where he slept, then stopped, hoping Maebh hadn't noticed.

Both beds were empty.

Gemm sucked in a deep breath. She stepped back into the hall. "Lo?" she called. They all knew there would be no answer.

A bang sounded from the kitchen. Mara jumped, and by the time she turned to find the source of the sound, Maebh and Gemm were already rushing down the stairs. She followed after them.

"Gemm? Are you here?" Lo stood just inside the cottage door, her chest heaving. "Is Noah gone?"

Even while she waited desperately for Lo's news, Mara felt a fresh wave of aching for Noah. She prodded their link and felt that rushing heat again. She told herself she would find him soon, and she tried her best not to think about the pain and fear and confusion that pulsed in him. She tried to believe he was not too badly hurt, and to ignore the part of herself that felt foolish for changing her mind about him so quickly.

Lo held out a dark leathery bundle, her face twisted with pain and sympathy, and all Mara's thoughts of Noah vanished. It was a sealskin—a youngling skin, years old and unused.

She snatched it from Lo's hands and clutched it to her chest, gasping. The scent was unmistakable. It was Aine's.

"Maebh," she said, her voice cracking. "Maebh —"

She uncoiled the skin, but something was wrong. It was too small, too light — the size of a newborn, not that of a youngling grown to her first change.

She dropped it, recoiling.

Maebh picked the skin up, cradling it as if it were Aine herself. "No," she said. "Oh, no."

It lay flat and unfurled in Maebh's arms, and they could all see the black scarring that edged it. The tail was still intact, but there was nothing left of the head or chest.

"Who could do this?" Maebh whispered, touching her finger to the scars, then pulling back with a wince. Mara knew that Maebh, too, was picturing the wounds on Aine's humanskin that would exactly match these.

"You didn't —" Mara hesitated, wondering if she or Maebh could bear any worse news. "You didn't find the — the other half, did you?"

Lo shook her head. "No. I mean . . ." She cleared her throat. Mara could tell she was trying to be gentle, but she was through with gentleness.

"What do you mean?" she demanded, her voice hoarse again.

"It's — um." Lo hesitated, and Gemm went to her and put a hand on her shoulder. She took a deep breath.

"Professor Foster's had it for a long time, and it looks like he's been . . . doing things to it." She stopped, closed her eyes, looked sick. "I think the rest of the skin is preserved, on slides, things like that. It's—it's in pieces."

Mara's stomach lurched. She ran to the sink, barely making it before her throat opened and she started to retch. Her stomach was empty, but thin bile leaked from her mouth, drooling into the sink, and the smell stung her eyes. She coughed and heaved, unable to stop herself, the picture of Aine's mutilated body unbearably clear in her mind.

She felt a cool hand on her forehead, stroking back her sweat-slicked hair. She managed to look up and saw Lo standing beside her.

"I know," she said quietly. "It's awful. It's more than awful. I'm so sorry." Still stroking Mara's hair, she turned and spoke to the rest of the room. "But Noah's gone, he went to Professor Foster's house with no one to help him. And Lir's there too, I'm sure of it, and maybe—maybe the girl, too. Ann?"

Maebh's voice wavered. "Aine."

"Right. Well, we have to go find them. We just have to."

Mara wiped her chin on a dishtowel. "You're right," she told Lo. "Let's go."

She felt a spike of fear from Maebh, but the Elder quieted her feelings and nodded. "Be safe, Mara," she said. She chuckled sadly. "I will not be able to deny it after this. You'll make a fine Elder, my daughter."

Mara couldn't bring herself to smile, but her heart thudded with relief. "I'll try," she whispered.

Lo glanced toward the door. "We can take the boat from the Center," she said. "It's as old as the *Minke* but it should get us there fine."

"Lo——" Gemm seemed about to protest, but then she shook her head. "Well. I let him go too, I suppose. Just—— please, be careful." She looked at Mara. "Both of you."

Mara nodded. "Let's go now," she said. "We can't waste any more time. They——" Her voice faltered.

Maebh stood and laid a hand on Mara's shoulder. "I know you can do this," she said. Mara pretended not to notice the fear in her voice, or on Gemm's face when she looked at her granddaughter.

She led Lo out the door and into the humid darkness, down the island's slope and onto the dock.

Her link with Noah throbbed with pain and fear. Mara cringed. "I'm coming," she whispered, even though she knew the link couldn't carry words. *I'm coming.*

thirty-four

Voice

AINE gasped. The feeling that broke over her skin was fierce, almost painful—as if a huge weight had lifted from her body and her muscles didn't know how to move without it. Her lungs convulsed and she coughed, deep wracking coughs that shook her ribs.

Lir touched her shoulder, and she looked up at him. His eyes were large and steady and frightened.

"It is all right," she whispered, and then she gasped again. She stood and backed against the wall, shaking harder still. She looked at her palms. A mist of blood was spattered over them where she'd covered her mouth.

"I—" She tried to speak. The sound of her voice moved through her ears like a stranger's.

She touched her fingers to her lips, prodded at her tongue and teeth and the soft insides of her cheeks. Her fingers were slick with red film when she looked at them again, but she didn't care.

For five years, even her screams had been silent.

"Aine," she whispered. She laughed, but that brought on another coughing fit, and she doubled over, shaking.

When she recovered, she wiped the tear tracks from her face and looked around the room. The young man was sprawled on the floor, his eyes closed. She felt a faint thread of understanding, of trust, emanating from him, as if she already knew him. The feeling was odd—something she could almost remember from the time before the fisherman.

She bent over him. His breaths were shallow, but his bleeding had started to slow.

"Who are you?" she murmured in his ear. "Why are you here?" Every word made her throat ache.

He groaned softly, and his eyes opened. "Noah," he said, his voice nearly as ragged as hers. "I'm here . . ." His eyes fluttered closed, then open. "I want to help you. Your sister—" He stopped, glancing toward the door.

Aine heard it too—the fisherman's steps on the stairs.

She leapt backwards, joining Lir in the corner. Noah closed his eyes and rested his head on the floor, so that it looked as if he hadn't woken.

She swallowed, pulling the taste of blood from her mouth. She curled into her body and shielded her face with her hair. Still, she was sure the fisherman would see the change in her.

Lir put his arm around her shoulders. They crouched

together as they'd done when the fisherman had first left them with the strange, injured boy.

Just as the door began to open, she thought she saw Noah nod toward them.

The fisherman opened the door so hard that it slammed against the wall. He pulled Noah's arms behind his back and tied them with a rope, tugging the ends tight.

He looked from the rope to Aine and Lir and then back, warning them. Aine's wrists ached with the memory of the ropes he'd used on her in the first year.

Eventually, the fisherman had learned that he didn't need the ropes. He had her skin, and that was enough to keep her docile—mostly. Aine had tried so many times to escape, or at least to hurt him back the way he'd hurt her, but she'd never managed anything more than a few bites when he fed her.

She watched the fisherman pace around the room, staring at Noah as if he didn't know what to do with him. His face was creased with worry or panic. He looked so weak, so confused, and she couldn't remember why she'd been so afraid all these years. She pressed her lips together to keep from laughing at him.

She watched Noah, wondering if he might have a plan to save them. But he'd barely been able to stay awake a few minutes ago, so she decided she and Lir were on their own.

Her legs tensed, and she felt her mouth start to open in

a snarl. She had her voice back now, and she was done with being docile. She wanted to attack.

The fisherman turned toward her and met her eyes. He twisted his key chain, the little circle of her skin clutched tight in his fist. She felt the pressure of his hand over the circular scar on her cheek. A tremor of fear returned, small, but enough to make her close her mouth and retreat into a crouch again.

Still, her mind raged to be free of him. She wanted to scream, just to show him she could. She bit the tip of her tongue to keep from crying out. Something was telling her to wait, to see what he would do before she struck.

She made herself tremble, entwined her arms with Lir's, and hitched her breath as if she were crying.

She felt Lir's hand move on her shoulder, and suddenly she didn't have to pretend to cry. Even with her voice returned, she had no words for the happiness of being reunited with her brother.

"Don't go anywhere," the fisherman said, facing Noah. He prodded Noah's bound arms with his foot. Worry washed over his face again, and he backed away, frowning. "I'll be right back." He closed the door behind him. The lock clicked into place.

Aine stood, pulling Lir up with her. "It is all right," she repeated.

Lir looked at the floor.

She walked to Noah and dug her fingers into the knots at his wrists. He pushed against the floor with his shoulder, wincing, and together they brought him up to lean against the wall.

"We have to be quiet," Noah reminded her.

She nodded, tugging at the rope. "I do not think I can do this," she whispered. The knots were thick and complicated, and she had never had to undo even a simple knot before. Her child's hands were short and stubby.

"Can you, um, bite it?" Noah looked at her apologetically, as if unsure whether he was being rude.

Aine grinned. She sank her teeth into the rope and sliced easily through its fibers. She knew she wouldn't have been able to defy the fisherman like this even an hour ago, and that knowledge made her savor the bitter taste of the rope on her tongue until she had bitten through the last knot.

Noah flexed his wrists, raw with rope burn. "Thank you." He craned his head around, trying to look at the wound on his back. His eyes fluttered and almost closed again. "Okay," he said. "I'm sorry, but I'm going to need your help." He breathed in, pressing one hand against the floor. He turned toward Lir. "Are you okay? Think you can help us?"

Lir blinked and opened his mouth, but no sound came out. His lips trembled.

"He cannot speak," Aine said. "I could not, either, until tonight."

Noah nodded. "Of course. Professor Foster still has his skin. I'd forgotten that part of the story."

"Story?" Aine wanted to hear what Noah knew about her kind, but as soon as she spoke, a realization came over her. "He—he doesn't have mine?"

"Not anymore." Noah's smile lit his tired face like daybreak. "Lo must have found it at the Center. I think you're free, Aine, or you will be, once we get out."

A thudding started between her ears, and it was several seconds before she recognized it as her own heartbeat. She took Noah's hand, once again feeling that echo of familiarity. "I am free," she said. "I feel it. I could feel it when it happened."

She hadn't held her sealskin yet, but no one was stopping her anymore. Even if she died trying to escape tonight —and well she might, she thought, remembering the fisherman's knife and the strength in his arms when he held her down—nonetheless, she was free.

Something crashed against the door.

"No!" A voice—a painfully familiar voice—screamed, and there was another crash. The wood on the much-abused door groaned, and its rusty hinges screeched.

"Mara?" Noah called, scrambling to his feet. He was shaking from blood loss, but he pulled hard on the door, bringing it a little closer to breaking open. He used his good arm, but his face still contorted with pain, and fresh blood pulsed from his shoulder — but only a little. Aine knew this kind of wound. She'd had hundreds of them, long and shallow and viciously bloody, the ones she gave herself on the windowsill or that appeared on their own when the fisherman did whatever-he-did with her faraway skin. They hurt and they certainly bled, but they stopped doing both soon enough. Those shallow wounds never kept her asleep as long as she wished they would.

But now her cuts were gone; she had only scars. Now she wanted to be awake.

They heard the fisherman yell. With a third crash, the lock broke and the door fell open.

The fisherman tumbled backwards into the room, howling and clutching his face. White liquid frothed out between his fingers.

Two women rushed through the doorway. The first had long, straight black hair, and at first Aine thought she was a selkie too. She ran to Noah right away, embracing him and crying out when she saw the gash in his back. She dropped the small black canister in her hand, and it spurted more whitish foam when it hit the floor.

Then Aine saw the second woman, and the first no longer mattered. She had black hair and eyes and the near-white skin of a selkie. She was older than she'd been when Aine had last seen her, but she knew her right away.

"Mara!" She tried to move but could not.

Mara knelt down in front of her and opened her arms, pulling Aine and Lir against her chest.

"Goddess," she whispered. "You're here; you're whole." She pulled back to look at them, and her face changed. She touched one of the ridged scars on Aine's face.

Aine flinched away.

"Oh, Aine," said Mara. "I'm not going to hurt you. I won't let anyone hurt you now." She reached toward another scar but stopped when she saw the way Aine looked at her.

"I'm sorry." Aine's fingers shook. She wrapped her arms tight around her torso and squeezed her hands into fists, but then her whole body began to shake. "I let him take me. I stayed here with him. It was my fault."

Mara stared at her. She shook her head. "No," she said, but Aine knew she was just trying to comfort her.

The other woman screamed, and Mara spun around to help her. The fisherman had found his knife again and had driven it into her ankle. She lay curled on the floor, clutching at her foot.

The fisherman rose, swiping the foam from his streaming eyes.

Mara pushed Aine and Lir back toward the wall. She sprang forward, jumping over the woman on the floor, and her hands closed over the fisherman's throat. She pinned him against the door frame.

"You won't hurt them again," she hissed. Her grip tightened and he gasped, his face darkening.

Mara bared her teeth and leaned toward his neck.

The fisherman choked and sputtered, but he still held the knife. He kept it out of Mara's sightline as he raised it over her back.

"Stop!" Noah pushed the dark-haired girl to the wall and lunged toward Mara. He hissed in pain and his shoulder jerked back, but he reached out and twisted the knife from the fisherman's fist. He clutched it by the blade, and when it dropped to the floor, it was slick with his blood.

Noah stood and braced his hands on the fisherman's chest, helping Mara keep him trapped against the door frame. His green eyes were dark with pain.

"You bastard," he growled. "I trusted you. I—Christ, I wanted to be you. How could you—how could you think any part of this was—" He stopped, shaking from loss of blood, and from anger, too. "They're people, Professor Foster. They're children."

The fisherman opened his mouth, but the only sound he could make was a strangled gurgle.

Aine met his eyes, watching him gulp hopelessly for air. It was good, seeing his voice stripped away as he'd stripped hers.

Mara loosened her fingers. For a moment Aine thought she wanted to let the fisherman speak, but then she opened her mouth, her teeth glinting white and sharp. She was going to tear out his throat.

"Mara." Aine slowly walked toward them. Her stomach revolted, remembering all the times he'd hurt her, but she could see how well Mara and Noah held him down. She knew he couldn't hurt her now.

Mara looked at her, still poised to attack. "He doesn't deserve your mercy, Aine." Her eyes followed the pattern of scars from Aine's hairline to her waist.

"I feel no mercy." Aine stared up at the fisherman, his face, as always, too high above her. She narrowed her eyes. "Sit."

Mara shoved him onto the floor. Noah knelt behind him and pinned the fisherman's hands to his back, leaving the red print of his palm on the older man's shirt. Mara moved in front of them, blocking them from Aine.

"Do not worry, Mara," she said. "You were right. He will never hurt me again."

Mara looked down at her for a long moment. Then she nodded reluctantly and joined Noah behind the fisherman, gripping the sides of his head between her hands.

"Try anything," she murmured in his ear, "and I'll snap your neck."

He nodded weakly. He stared up at Aine, waiting for the blow.

She ran her tongue along her closed teeth, imagining

them slicing through his windpipe. But the idea of touching him repulsed her. He had never left her untouched, in all these years. Her scars were proof of that. She never wanted to feel his skin on hers again.

She inhaled deeply. She'd wished for speech for so long, to tell him to set her free, to tell him to stop. What could she possibly say to him now that would do justice to all that forced silence?

"Hope," he wheezed, his face growing pale. "My Hope. I'm so sorry."

She met his eyes. She knew what to say to him now.

"My name is not Hope." She ran her hands up over her face, the lines of scarring like fish scales under her fingers, and pushed back the long weight of her hair. "And I am not yours."

She crouched and clutched the bloody knife that lay beside Noah. He looked at her doubtfully, but he didn't stop her.

She held the point of the knife to the fisherman's face. He swallowed.

"Every time you cut me"—she pressed the point closer to his cheek, not quite hard enough to break his skin—"I watched the wounds grow. I felt your blade." She shivered, then pushed in the point of the knife. A drop of red grew at the fisherman's cheekbone. "I felt your tongue and your teeth."

Mara let out a low bark, and her hands jerked. Noah

sent her a steadying look, and she nodded and grew still. Her eyes shone wet.

Aine adjusted her grip on the knife. She pulled the blade up, drawing a circle of split flesh that matched her oldest scar.

His jaw tightened as she cut. He flinched, but he made no sound. His eyes were swollen and red.

Aine pulled the knife away. "I will not kill you," she said. She ignored Mara's growl of protest. "You could have killed me, I think, and kept my skin, but you did not." She finished the circle and stepped back. "But I will not leave you unmarked."

She dropped the knife and watched him bleed.

The room was silent.

She looked behind her, to where Lir stood in the corner. The circle mark on his cheek stood out darkly in the moonlight brimming in from the window. He touched a hand to his slim throat.

The dark-haired human moved toward the door, wincing after every hobbling step. She turned and looked back at them. "I think—I'm just going to bandage this up."

Noah nodded. "I'll help you, Lo."

Lo shook her head. "I can do this myself. Help them." She looked at Aine. "I can manage." She limped down the stairs.

Aine waited for Mara and Noah to exit next, but Mara shook her head.

"I want to see you walk outside," she said. "I know how long you've waited."

Aine stared into the hall. She stepped forward, and her heartbeat sped up, careening through her body. The fisherman's legs were sprawled between her and the doorway.

She glanced at him, at the only room she had known for five years. The chipped, worn-down windowsill, the stained walls — they were so familiar. She could hardly remember anything else.

She told her feet to keep moving, but they would not.

"It's okay," Mara said. She turned toward Noah. "Have you got him?"

He nodded, his face still pale and his jaw tight.

Mara stood, releasing the fisherman's head. She gathered Lir up from his corner, holding him against her hip and letting his head rest on her shoulder. She reached out to Aine. "I can carry you."

Aine shook her head fiercely. She stared at the doorway. To have wanted it for so long, not to have wanted anything else . . . and then to get it, the impossible thing . . . To have it simply handed to her like this felt wrong, somehow. She hadn't earned the right to walk out that door.

She looked back at the fisherman, at his bloodied face, and a shudder spread from the base of her spine all through her body. She could feel her hair quivering against her back, the shaky hold of her toes on the floor. Her knees locked, her legs cramped, and she felt herself starting to fall.

She spread out her arms and hands, the tips of her fingers jerking, and steadied herself. She sensed the pod's links in her, pulling her toward freedom, toward their love, and they helped her stand. She closed her eyes, and in that moment she could feel the rhythm of the sea.

When she opened them again, she was a step closer to the door. Mara came up behind her, still carrying Lir, and held out her hand.

Aine grasped it, and her sense of the links strengthened. Together, they walked out into the hallway.

She looked back one more time, and saw Noah pick up the knife and stand over the fisherman, the man he'd called Foster.

"You didn't deserve that," Noah told him. "You deserved so much worse. I know you won't tell anyone about this, since you've kept Aine a secret for so long. But if you do, if you ever tell anyone," he said, his voice cold, "I will kill you."

The fisherman dropped his head, staring between his knees. Aine thought she heard him mumble yes.

"And Lir's skin?"

"The boy?" Foster took another ragged breath. "Basement. Behind the stairs. You'll find it."

He dug the key chain out of his pocket and held it out, his hand trembling like that of a much older man.

Noah took it, pulling off the two circles of sealskin, one worn smooth, the other still bloody, before stuffing the key chain in his pocket. Aine felt the pull at her cheek, and she knew Lir would feel it too.

He stared at the circles in his hand, and the fisherman stayed still, watching him. Noah's voice, when he spoke again, was quiet and sad. "Don't you know how much I admired you—how good I thought you were?"

The fisherman took a shaky breath. "You don't understand."

Noah's head jerked up and his eyes flashed. "Don't under— Of course I don't."

"The skin. It does things. It did things to me. It can make you well, make you younger. It's worth so much more this way."

Noah looked at Aine, then back at the fisherman. "Worth?" He put the circles in his pocket, but Aine could feel that he claimed no ownership of them. He tossed the knife into the corner of the room. He balled his hand into a fist, pulled back, and punched the fisherman so hard, he fell sideways to the floor. His eyes rolled back, showing only white, and then they closed.

"In case he wanted to follow us," Noah said casually. He joined them in the hallway.

Downstairs, the girl named Lo waited for them in the kitchen. She had tied a ragged strip of fabric, torn from her shirt, around her ankle to stanch the bleeding.

"You need a doctor," said Noah, his face tight with worry again.

Lo nodded reluctantly. "I'll call an ambulance," she said. "You need to get them home while it's still dark, so no one sees."

Noah started to protest, but Lo went on. "I have this whole story worked out for them. Professor Foster invited me here, like he invited you a while ago." She looked at Noah. "And then he attacked me, locked me up in that room. I just barely managed to get away." She touched her ankle, then looked up at Aine. "He could use some jail time, if you ask me."

She took something small and black out of her pocket. She touched it, and it blinked into glowing life. "The GPS says the hospital's just a few minutes from here. I'll be fine."

Noah frowned. "How'd you get this address, anyway?"

Lo rolled her eyes. "We have his forwarding address in the filing room's server. You're a little dumb sometimes, you know."

He sighed. "I don't want to leave you here alone."

"Yeah, well. Too bad."

They stared at each other for a long moment. Finally he shrugged and chuckled a little. "Christ, you're stubborn. Call from the hospital, okay?"

"Okay." Lo hugged Noah, squeezing her arms tight around him. She looked up at him and smiled. "I'm glad you're not dead."

Noah laughed, the sound hollow. "Yeah. Me, too."

He left for a few minutes, and came back holding Lir's

skin. It had a circle cut from it, just like the circle of Aine's skin the fisherman — Foster, Noah had called him — had first taken from her. She reached up and stroked the round scar on her cheek.

They left just as Lo called for the ambulance, so they wouldn't be there to contradict her story. Aine could smell the ocean as soon as they opened the door. She heard the hushed breaths of the waves, and her pounding heart matched their rhythm.

Noah led them down the road from the fisherman's house to the docks. The boat was there waiting for them, but when Aine saw the water, she could think of nothing but how it would feel on her skin.

She didn't realize she'd tried to jump from the dock until she felt Mara's hands restraining her. "Wait," she said. "Wait until we get home. It's too dangerous here."

Aine let out a wail, an uncontrolled babyish sound that embarrassed her even as she made it. She needed the water. She needed it.

Mara's arms encircled her. "Soon," she said. "So soon, I promise."

Aine made herself nod, though her skin still ached with desire for cold and salt and sea. She leaned back in Mara's arms and took in a deep, shaky breath.

Noah waited for them in the boat. Mara lifted first Aine and then Lir over the side, and Noah nestled them each into white seats with thin, soft cushions.

Mara leapt in after them. She and Noah unhitched the ropes that held the boat to the docks. She stood behind Aine and Lir, one hand on each of their shoulders, and they watched Noah maneuver the boat out of its berth and into the harbor. The engine purred softly under Aine's seat, and the boat shot fast and smooth through the deepening water.

Noah stared ahead, his back straight and his hands firm on the wheel, despite the wound that still dampened the back of his shirt with blood.

Mara moved forward and joined him. For several minutes she just stood there, looking out to the horizon with him. Her hand, though, inched toward his.

He winced when her littlest finger brushed the side of his palm. He looked at her, his eyes bright and questioning, and then back at the ocean ahead.

"I knew nothing," he said quietly. "I would never have done that to you."

"I know." Mara's fingers twined over his. "I'm sorry."

He leaned into her, keeping one hand on the wheel.

Aine felt her link with Mara grow warmer.

A gray smudge appeared on the horizon, followed by another, and then another. Aine pushed herself up in her seat, trying to see them better. Soon she could make out buildings: an old chapel, a hotel, the white pillar of the lighthouse.

The Isles of Shoals grew before her, dark and rocky, calling her home.

thirty-five

CHANGE

Maebh and Gemm were waiting for them on the shore of White Island. As soon as Noah pulled up to the dock, Maebh ran to the *Minke*, tears streaming over her face.

"Aine, Lir—" She jumped into the boat. Lir embraced her eagerly, but Aine shied away, wrapping her hair over her chest like a shield. The scars on her arms glinted gray in the fading moonlight.

Maebh nodded and backed away, but Mara hated the unfulfilled longing that welled in their link. She offered Maebh her own embrace, though she knew it would not be enough.

As they parted, Noah stepped toward them and reached into his pocket. He took out the two circles of sealskin, one worn and one raw, and laid them delicately across his palm.

"It might be best if Maebh . . ." he said.

Mara nodded. She lifted the circles carefully from his hand. "They were like totems for him, I think," she said to Maebh. "I don't know if they're any use to the children now."

The Elder looked down. She nodded slowly, sadly.

"They should have these back once they're less frightened," she said. "Surely they'll remind them of — him. I will take them for now." Maebh's head bowed; she stroked one cautious finger across each circle, then put them gently in her tunic pocket. Mara knew Maebh wished she could touch Aine the same way — but only Aine would decide who touched her now.

"She's been through so much," Mara reminded the Elder.

"I know," Maebh said. "We must not press her too hard." But her voice trembled.

Mara pulled back, searching Maebh's face. "Can you get her skin?" she asked. "I think it might help her to have it back, even if . . ." She remembered the spent look of Aine's half-skin.

Maebh nodded. She beckoned to Lir. He ran to her, his skin clutched tight under one arm, and she hoisted him up so he could wrap his legs around her waist. She lumbered up the dock with him, over the rocky ground to the crest of the island, and into the cottage.

Gemm took a rope to make the boat fast to the dock, and Noah stepped out to help her.

"Where's Lo?" Her eyes darted toward the ocean.

"She went to the hospital," said Noah, "but she's okay, Gemm, I swear." He laid a hand on his grandmother's shoulder, but she saw the blood on his shirt and made a noise of protest.

"You should have gone with her. What on earth did he do to you?"

Noah shook his head, curling his other hand into a loose fist so she wouldn't see the cut there. "Really, Gemm, it's not that bad," he insisted as she exclaimed over the blood. "I can still move my arm just fine—see? It was a lot of blood, I know, but the cut's not that deep." He pulled his shirt off, wincing as he raised his arm over his head. He turned around and showed her his back, the wound jagged across his sleek runner's muscles.

Gemm took Noah's shirt from him and used it to gently wipe some of the blood away. She raised her eyebrows. "I'm surprised you didn't pass out," she muttered.

Noah scoffed, but Mara felt a tinge of embarrassment in their link. "I'm tougher than I look, I guess."

"Well, now, of course you are." Gemm smiled. "At least let me bandage it for you. There's some antiseptic in the medicine cabinet." She bustled off toward the cottage.

"She's right, you know," said Mara, joining Noah at the boat's side. "You're lucky it wasn't much worse." Her fingers wandered out, brushing against the bare skin of his lower back.

Someone behind them cleared her throat. Mara jumped backwards, embarrassed, as if she'd been caught doing something private.

She turned to see Maebh walking toward them with Aine's mutilated skin. Lir followed her, his own skin clutched tightly in his arms. Gemm came last, carrying a small white box.

Aine stared at her skin from the boat, shaking again.

Maebh stepped toward her, but Aine backed to the starboard edge. "I—I want Mara," she said.

Maebh looked down for a moment, her smile breaking. When she looked up, her expression was calm and unmarred. She held the skin out to Mara. "Should I get yours, too?" she asked.

"No," Mara said. "Aine might need me to hold her up."

Aine looked out at the waves. She chewed on her lips, tonguing the thick scar that ran down their center and extended over her chin and neck. She wrapped her arms around her body and shook her head.

Mara climbed back into the boat and knelt beside her sister. "It's all right," she said. "You've been so brave, Aine. You don't have to do this right now if you don't want to."

Aine kept her eyes on the water. "I do. I—I want to. But it scares me, that I had forgotten about the ocean."

It was strange—Aine looked no older than Lir or any other youngling at her first change. But the way she spoke and the sound of her voice were much older, almost adult. She carried herself like an old woman, her hands shaking, her shoulders hunched.

Mara closed those hands softly in her own, wishing she could still them. "Just follow me," she said. She stood, and without letting go, she moved backwards off the dock.

Aine followed, hardly looking where she stepped, her eyes locked with Mara's. At the shoreline, she pulled her hands away and began to walk on her own.

The tide was almost slack, the ocean nearly quiet. Small waves lipped onto the shore. The edges of the sky grayed with the end of night.

Aine winced when the first ripple crept over her toes. She was still wearing an old white shirt of Professor Foster's, and it dipped into the water with every slow step, its hem growing wet and heavy. As she walked deeper into the water, it rose around her, drifting in the waves like a round white flower.

When she turned back toward them she was smiling, pushing her arms against the currents, almost swimming. "See me, Maebh?" she called, a hint of childhood in her voice again.

"Yes, Aine, I see you." Maebh's voice hitched, and Gemm left her ministrations at Noah's shoulder to come stand by her side. The Elder brushed her hand over Lir's dark hair.

Mara walked into the water and dipped Aine's skin below the surface. The dry cracks it had accumulated from years on land softened, and she could feel them starting to heal. But they would not mend completely, she knew, unless Aine could change. She saw Maebh's face, tight with worry, and she shared her fear. So little of the skin was left.

Aine waded toward her and held out her shaking hands for the skin.

"Feet first, remember," said Mara, trying to sound as if she couldn't imagine the change failing.

Aine pulled off her shirt and dropped it into the water. She swam closer, and Mara caught her under her arms, holding her head above the water while she pushed her feet into the sealskin. She could feel everyone on shore holding their breath.

Aine shuddered in her grasp. The skin slithered over her knees, then wound past her thighs and up to the childish line of her waist. It curled over the humanskin below her navel, knitting into her flesh, and stopped.

It was clear it could reach no farther.

Mara thought she would cry. It was foolish to have thought the change would work, she knew. But now Aine could never really change.

Aine twisted around to look at her. Her eyes were wide, and the trembling in her body was fading. The scarred corners of her mouth rose in a smile.

"I think . . ." She closed her eyes, listening for something inside herself. "I think I'm growing again, Mara. I think I'm getting older, now."

"It's the change," said Maebh, wading toward them. "Every time you change, you'll grow a little older." She held out her arms, her face tight with hope.

Aine swam toward her. She reached out to grasp Maebh's

hands, but just before they touched, she winced and pulled back.

"I can't," she said. "I don't know why, but I just . . . can't have everyone touch me right now."

Mara tried to ignore the jealousy simmering in Maebh's link. She didn't understand, either, but she knew they had to give Aine time. She tried to offer Maebh a sense of patience.

"Do whatever you need to, Aine," Maebh said. "The important thing is that you're home now."

Aine looked out to sea. She ducked her head under and swam away from them, aiming for the open ocean beyond Gosport Harbor.

"Oh —" Maebh's link filled with fear.

But soon Aine circled around and returned to them. She was panting as her head emerged from the water. "They're coming," she said, her voice high and shrill.

A line of dark, slick forms cut through the waves: Ronan and the younglings. Mara stepped in front of Aine, worried that they were all going to tackle her at once.

But the younglings hung back, shy. Mara realized they might not remember much of their lost sister. Only Ronan swam right up to them. He changed as he rose out of the water, his sealskin sliding down from his head in sticky folds.

"Aine," he said, reaching past Mara.

"Careful, Ronan," Mara warned. "She's still over-whelmed."

Aine stared up at Ronan. "I remember you," she said. "I missed you the most, Brother."

The muscles in Ronan's shoulders twitched, and Mara knew it was all he could do not to swing her up in his arms. But he was better with the younglings than either she or Maebh, and he seemed to understand why he couldn't touch her. "I missed you, too," he said.

Four youngling heads popped up behind Ronan. Mara smiled at what she felt in their links, the overwhelming curiosity drowning out their shyness. She heard a splash behind her and watched Lir run into the waves, tripping as he struggled to pull on his sealskin and join his siblings.

"This is hard," he said, scowling at his skin.

Ronan turned to help him, but Aine was there first. "Wait," she said. "Breathe for a moment. You have to want it, have to want the change."

Lir closed his eyes; the muscles in his face softened. Aine put a hand on his arm. "Yes, that way."

Ronan and Mara looked at each other, surprise and pleasure meeting in their links.

The other younglings, seeing her kindness to Lir, began to approach Aine. They circled around her, sniffing the air and gauging their links. The circle began to move out to sea, and Aine moved with them at its center, until they were racing out to Whale Rock together, spinning and tumbling under the waves.

Ronan turned away and swam after the younglings, and Mara heard his laugh turn into a seal's bark as he chased them.

A ringing sounded on the shore, and Gemm pulled a black rectangle like Lo's from her pocket. "Oh—" She pressed it to her ear. "Lo, honey? Are you all right?" She started walking back toward the cottage, and Maebh followed. "Oh, good. Oh, thank goodness."

Mara waded over to the dock. Noah was waiting for her, holding out his hand to help her climb up. She gave him a look, just to make sure he knew she could do it by herself, then took his hand and smiled.

She settled next to him, and they dangled their legs into the water. She looked at his face, then down at her hands, not knowing what to say.

Noah was quiet too, and she felt a weariness in him even deeper than her own. She could barely fathom how only yesterday they'd set off for the Midsummer dance in Gemm's boat. She felt as if months had passed in the hours of that night.

Finally, Noah broke the silence. "Aine is like a mermaid now, isn't she?"

Mara looked out to Whale Rock and saw her there, a pale streak among the dark seal forms of the other younglings. "Not really." She looked at him, amused. "Do you think so?"

"Of course, I mean, the tail, the . . ." He trailed off. A slow smile grew on his face, and his link vibrated with excitement. "Wait. Are you saying she's not like a mermaid because — because those are real too? Have you seen one?"

Mara smiled. "No. Maebh told us stories about people like that — sirens — but the way she talked about them, I always figured they were *only* stories." She shrugged, not wanting to disappoint him. "Maybe there are real ones in some other part of the world. But selkies don't know of them — at least, our pod doesn't — and they probably don't know of us, either."

He scooted a little closer to her. "Good. It's nice to know some things are mysteries to you, too."

They were quiet again, but their silence was more comfortable than it had been before. The sun was beginning to rise in front of them. Waves slid onto the shore like stroking fingers.

"Gemm was right," Noah said after several minutes had passed.

"What do you mean?" Mara glanced toward him and immediately saw the white bandage on his back. "Oh."

"It could have been way worse, you know? I mean, I should have been so much more afraid. And I was afraid." He frowned, remembering. "But I could tell you were coming, Mara. I could feel it."

He slipped his arm around her and drew her close.

She nestled into him, resting her head under his chin. She took a deep breath; when she exhaled, her lips brushed the indent under his throat. Their link sparked. She smiled and tried it again, kissing him more purposefully.

Noah touched her chin, urging her face upward. She looked in his eyes, suddenly embarrassed at the heat in her. They were linked. He would feel everything she felt.

He stroked her cheek with his thumb, his eyes somber. His other arm clasped tighter around her back, and he bent his head and kissed her.

Mara leaned back onto the dock, sliding a hand into Noah's hair and pulling him down with her. He flinched when his injured shoulder met the wood. Mara pushed herself up with her hands. Had she hurt him?

He shook his head no before she could ask. He touched the side of her face again and brought her down for another kiss.

The first sunlight touched the dock, warming the wood and her skin. Mara could feel her wet clothes starting to dry in the morning air. Each moment brought more light, and she knew that soon everyone on the Shoals would be able to see them.

Noah took her lower lip between his and sucked on it gently, his hands tightening on her hips. Mara forgot about anyone who might be watching and put all her attention into kissing him back.

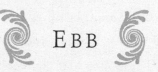

thirty-six

EBB

LO tapped the end of her pencil against the clipboard in her hand. The Center had been a disorganized mess ever since Professor Foster's "absence," as everyone was calling it. It had been almost a month, and things still weren't back to normal. Lo quickly discovered that none of the research staff was particularly interested in the paperwork necessary to keep the Center running smoothly.

It wasn't that Lo was so eager to do it, either, but the new director had offered her actual *money*, and Lo was suddenly too busy picturing all the art supplies she could buy with the money to say no. Besides, she liked making sure everything was in its rightful place. She was learning how nice it was to be in control of something.

Thinking of that, she decided it was time to set Professor Foster's office to rights. They had destroyed all the dead sealskin samples, everything really dangerous, as soon as they could, but the mundane scattered *mess* of it all was something they'd decided they could deal with later, when they had all recovered. Well, later had come, and Lo found that — as usual — she was the one cleaning the boring bits up. The new director would be on-site in a week, and it had to be spotless by then — it was a snowdrift of loose papers at the moment. The police had chalked up its disorder to Professor Foster's "mental breakdown," but Lo knew better.

She set her clipboard down on top of a stack of back issues of *Aquatic Conservation*. She glanced around the room and realized she had no idea where to start. She'd really made a mess of this place.

She remembered prying open desk drawers and pulling out reams of paper and whole sets of slides. Thinking of the story Gemm had told her about the selkie and the fisherman, she had even looked up at the ceiling, hoping for rafters.

But it was in the file cabinet, at last, that she'd found Aine's skin. She decided to start her cleanup work there.

Rifling through the lab reports and scribbled-over legal pads, she remembered the odd pulsing warmth of that skin in her hands. It had looked so dead, dry and cracked and folded as it was, but it had felt *alive*.

She'd seen Aine in it several times now. The girl was still shy around humans, of course, but for some reason, she was a little more comfortable around Lo than around Gemm or Noah.

She thought back to a few days ago, when she had settled down on Gemm's dock to make sketches of the Oceanic

Hotel from a distance, of the patterns the lights made on the ocean when the sun rose. Aine had appeared in the water in front of her.

Lo had waved shyly, pencil still between her fingers, and Aine had waved back. After a few moments of silent observing, Aine had put a hand on the dock and asked, "Can I see what you're doing?"

Surprised, Lo had nodded, smiling.

Aine looked around them, checking for boats, then pulled herself up onto the dock and sat next to Lo. Small rivers of seawater slid over her skin and tail and pooled in dark circles on the wood. She closed her eyes for a moment, concentrating, then gripped the skin of her tail and slipped it down and off. Her legs, free of the scars that etched her upper body, looked almost as if they belonged to someone else.

"Are you sure there's no one around?"

Aine looked down at her legs. "I checked. It's so early, anyway." She folded her skin and placed it next to her on the dock, near a gray sweater Lo had cast off because the day was so warm. Aine glanced at the sweater. "Do you mind if I . . ." She trailed off.

Lo shook her head. "Of course not. Go for it."

Aine squeezed the extra water out of her hair and coiled it over her shoulder. Its ends brushed the dock. She wiggled into the sweater and smiled at Lo. "Thanks," she said. "Just right." She leaned over to see Lo's half-finished sketch.

"Oh," she said, her smile brightening. "It looks just the same! But . . ." She squinted at the hotel, then back at the page. "But better. It's the way you see it, not the way it is."

Lo looked at the girl next to her, and in spite of the sealskin on the dock, the little child's body, the scars that hinted at pain Lo couldn't even imagine, her heart leapt out and ached with recognition for the kindred spirit next to her.

"Have you ever drawn before?"

Aine shook her head.

"I could teach you. If you want."

After that day, they had spent nearly every morning like that, drawing together on the dock, until Lo had to go to work.

She tapped a stack of paper against the desk to straighten it, then slid it into a file in the cabinet's top drawer.

She hardly thought of the selkies as separate from her own family anymore. There was Maebh, who spent almost every night on White Island now. She was turning into the perfect grandmother, even if she did look so much younger than Gemm.

And then, of course, there was Mara. The way Noah looked at her was . . . Well, it was gross for Lo to think about it. But there was tenderness there too, a deepness between them when they spoke to each other, that filled Lo with a certain contentment. If her brother had to be in love, she was glad it was with someone who obviously loved him back just as much.

She had no idea what they were going to do at the end of the summer, but she wasn't looking forward to dealing with a post-Mara Noah. At least he'd be busy packing for college when they got back to their parents' house, and soon . . . soon, he would leave.

Lo blinked. For a moment, the papers in her hands went blurry. She was looking forward to Noah's leaving for college. When had that happened? Only a few months ago she had wished desperately that they were closer in age so that he could stay home a little longer to help her deal with their parents. And a few months before that, she would have given anything for him just to get out of the house and leave her alone.

This was different. She didn't want Noah gone for those reasons anymore. She just knew he would be in pain, once they left the Shoals and the selkies behind, and she couldn't bear to see that. She didn't want that for him.

Lo shook her head and turned toward Professor Foster's disheveled desk. Between Gemm and Maebh, and Mara and Noah, she was beginning to wonder whether love was worth the heartache.

thirty-seven

 HARBOR

MARA and Ronan were the only ones who had managed to change, and they each had two younglings in hand, trying to help pull off their sealskins. The first season was always difficult for younglings, Mara knew, but she couldn't remember ever having such a hard time turning human herself.

"Lir, stay still." She grasped his right foot—the only part of him that wasn't seal—and tugged. A human leg appeared, up to the knee. "Good."

Lir growled, frustrated, but his other leg slipped out of his sealskin next to the first. Mara watched as all at once his skin split to the crown of his head and he emerged, pale in the darkness, a slightly damp but otherwise passably human young boy.

"See my dreads, Mara? Ronan did them for me, last time I was human." Lir shook his head, and his narrow, shoulder-length dreadlocks twirled.

"Very nice. Will you be okay walking up to the cottage by yourself, or do you want to wait for the others?"

He replied by pulling the old T-shirt Mara held away

from her and over his head. He grabbed his sealskin from the ground and sprinted up to the cottage door. "Noah!" he yelled. "We're here!"

Mara glanced at Ronan just in time to see him shake his head. Despite what had happened to him, Lir had taken to the humans a bit more than the other younglings had. Ronan, though usually civil, could still hardly bring himself to think well of them.

"Remember, they brought Aine back to us," Mara said, holding her hands out to help him pull Branna out of her sealskin.

"Yes," he agreed, his voice even gruffer than usual. "Of course, they took her away in the first place."

Mara bit back the growl that suddenly rose in her throat. She tried to make herself see things his way. After all, she had once thought the same thing.

"These people had nothing to do with that. You know that, Ronan. And look at Maebh, at how much she loves Gemm. You wouldn't take that happiness from her, would you?"

Ronan looked in her eyes, and a flicker of kindness showed itself in their link. "No, Mara. I wouldn't deny her that."

Something in his voice made her blush and look away. "Well, good, then. Let's get them inside."

When all the younglings had managed their changes and wriggled into hand-me-down Gallagher clothes, Mara waved them toward the cottage. Ronan herded them from behind.

Aine was already inside, seated next to Lo at the table. The two of them had grown close in the last weeks, and Mara was trying to keep from being jealous. It made sense, she reminded herself, that they would want to spend time together. Though Aine still had the body of a child, she and Lo were actually close to the same age.

And if she were truly honest with herself, Mara knew that Aine still didn't feel at home with the pod. She couldn't hunt with them, because her human lungs lacked the capacity to keep her underwater for more than a minute or so. She was a strong swimmer, but she was still getting used to the contradictions of her half-seal, half-human body, and she was not yet as fast or as graceful in the water as her siblings, or as protected from cold water and weather as they were. Worst of all, she could not hide in her seal form the way the others could. Any human who saw her would immediately know her for what she was—or at least, would make a close-enough guess. Mermaid or selkie, Aine was not safe when she wore her sealskin. Of course it made sense that she would spend more time on land.

Still, Mara worried about the life that lay ahead for Aine. Lo would leave soon—*Noah*, *too*, her mind whispered, but Mara shoved that thought away—and then Aine would be left alone, caught in limbo, neither seal nor human. Forever.

She felt a tingle of sympathy enter her body, and she noticed Maebh looking at her. The Elder's link told her that everything would turn out well, but Mara was having trouble believing it.

The younglings crowded together on the floor, piling against one another just as they did when they were seals. Lir was by the couch, leaning against Noah's shin. His eyes darted between his siblings and his new idol. Ever since their rescue, Lir had adored Noah, following him whenever he could and telling the other younglings exaggerated stories about him.

Ronan glared at them, and Mara touched his arm. She thought Lir's devotion to Noah was charming, but she could understand how Ronan might feel uneasy and possessive about it. That was exactly the way she felt about Lo and Aine.

Ronan looked at her, and she tried to send him some measure of patience or empathy. He nodded grudgingly, and she slipped away from him and sat down with Noah.

Noah shifted and laid his arm over the back of the couch, not quite touching her. Still, she could feel the comforting circle of him around her. She settled back, the muscles of her shoulders relaxing for the first time since . . . since the last time she'd seen him. That had been only yesterday, she knew, but it felt like much longer. Once more she pushed away the knowledge that he would leave her soon.

"Is everyone here?" asked Gemm.

"Everyone." Mara reached down and stroked Lir's dreadlocks.

"Well, then." Gemm took the lid off a large metal pot on the stove. Fragrant steam drifted into the room. "Dinner is served."

The younglings crowded up to her first. They'd eaten human food only a few times, but they found the concept of hot, cooked meals endlessly fascinating. Mara did too — the spices, the herbs, the simmering and roasting and baking — it was so complex. The only decision they had to make as seals was which kind of fish to hunt on a given night.

Aine stayed to one side, watching her brothers and sisters wait for their dinner. After Gemm had ladled out chowder for each of them, she dug through the refrigerator and pulled out a small tuna steak. She unwrapped the plastic film around it and laid it neatly on a plate.

"Here you go, sweetie," she said.

Aine took the fish and ate with her hands, her teeth tearing through the raw flesh. She couldn't stand human food, and none of them felt the slightest need to force it on her.

Mara told herself to stop worrying about Aine. There were hard things ahead for her, she was sure, but for now she was safe.

Mara looked around the tiny cottage, filled almost to bursting with everyone she loved. Perhaps the pod would never be safe again, now that humans knew about them. Perhaps Aine would never fully recover. But now, at this moment, she didn't want to think of those things. She tucked herself closer to Noah, feeling utterly certain that she was home.

thirty-eight

 # LAND AND SEA

NOAH had no idea how this had gotten so out of control. He stared at the piles of clothes and books that flooded his half of the bedroom, knowing his bags would have to be packed, and his room restored to its original neatness, by tomorrow. He just couldn't make himself believe that he was really leaving.

Beyond the folding screen, Lo's coordinated purple luggage lay stacked by the door. Even her bed was neatly made, the sheets tucked so tight into the mattress that they were probably bulletproof.

Lo herself had been on Appledore all day, taking yet another extra shift to help keep the Center running smoothly until the new director arrived. It was just like her to have everything organized and ready to go with a day to spare. Noah thought back to what Lo's therapist had told their parents about eating disorders and about how she needed to be in control of something. She seemed to be starting to channel that need in better ways, but he knew it would take a long time to know for sure. He was just thankful that right now she seemed healthy, happy, free from the trap her body used to be for her.

He slumped back onto his bed. He didn't *feel* as if he were leaving tomorrow — maybe that was his problem. If he could just convince himself that the summer was really over . . .

His mind recoiled from that train of thought, and he was left staring blankly at the unzipped duffle bag on his bed. He couldn't let himself believe that he was leaving the Shoals, because that meant he'd be leaving Mara, too.

That spark — their link — opened up inside him, and he could feel her nearby, as if she'd been waiting for him to think of her. They'd both been so busy, he'd hardly felt the link at all over the past few days, and he'd almost forgotten the physical pull it had on him.

Noah rose from the bed and walked downstairs, knowing he could hardly have resisted responding to the link, even if he'd wanted to. He thought he would never understand how Gemm had ignored it for so many years before returning to Maebh.

His two grandmothers sat at the table downstairs, murmuring urgently to each other. They quieted as soon as Noah appeared on the steps.

A sealskin lay folded near Maebh's elbow, but it wasn't hers. Noah squinted at it, and shuddered when he realized it was Aine's. Seeing her scarred, too-small skin always brought back the memory of Professor Foster's house, always woke up the pain in his still-healing wounds.

Ever since their rescue, he hadn't seen Aine without her skin—she wouldn't even hide it the way the others did, but carried it with her. She changed several times a day, trying to speed up her growth so her body's age would match her mind's. He couldn't imagine how Maebh had separated the girl from her sealskin—or why she would even want to.

"Packed yet, honey?" asked Gemm, tearing her gaze away from Maebh's.

Noah cleared his throat. "Um, I'm getting there, I guess."

Gemm laughed. "All right, well, the ferry leaves Star at nine a.m. tomorrow, remember."

Noah nodded, walking faster to get out of the cottage and away from any talk about leaving.

But outside, there were other reminders that summer was ending. The grass was brown and stiff, dried out by months of salt spray and heat. The waves broke hurriedly over themselves, foamy and pale. There was a warm, earthy scent over everything, like the smell of dry leaves on the mainland.

And there was Mara, waiting for him on the rocks beyond the lighthouse. He could see her smiling, but she carried the same knowledge Noah did: this was their last day together.

She took his hand. They walked to the very edge of the island, where the granite boulders turned steep, worn vertical with eons of waves. The lighthouse flashed above them, but in the daytime Noah could hardly distinguish its beam from the glare of the sun.

"Let's stay here." Mara folded herself onto the ground and dangled her feet over the cliff's edge.

Noah joined her, looking down at the crashing waves beneath them and thinking of the other times he'd been on this part of the island with Mara. He'd learned she was a selkie here, leaning over the cliffs and watching her shed her sealskin. She'd attacked him on those rocks when she'd thought he'd hurt Lir.

Mara cringed away from him. "I'm sorry about that," she said.

It took a moment for Noah to remember their link. She could read only his feelings, not his thoughts, he knew — but it was easy for him to forget how much the two over-lapped.

"It's okay." He slipped his arm around her waist. "I know why you did it."

He felt something rise inside her — excitement and pride. He waited for her to tell him what it was, but she only chewed her lip and was silent.

"What is it, Mara?"

She smiled. "Maebh told the pod last night. She's made me Elder."

Noah's chest tightened. He had to turn away for a moment, to rearrange the look on his face. "That's great."

He didn't know why it should matter to him. She would never leave the Shoals now — but, he reminded himself, he would never have asked that of her. Of course not.

"Noah." He felt Mara's fingers on his hair, gently urging him to turn and look at her. "I've wanted this my whole life."

"I know." Noah shook his head, ignoring the extra liquid at the corners of his eyes. "Really, Mara, it's great. I'm just—" He sighed. "I just want too many different things."

"I know." She leaned against him. "Me, too."

They watched the seals slide off Whale Rock, then dive and return to the surface with fat, silvery fish in their jaws.

"Aine needed a full skin, you see," she said.

Noah nodded, even though he didn't see at all how that would make Maebh give up the pod to Mara.

"And Maebh and your grandmother, they lost so much time with each other. So Aine is taking Maebh's skin, and Maebh will live here with Gemm, and I'll lead the pod. They'll be together, always."

So many different feelings glimmered through her link when she said that, Noah couldn't read any of them.

She straightened her back, still watching the pod. "I really think I can help them," she went on. "We'll have the moon ceremonies here, on White, where Maebh and Gemm can help guard them from . . ." She glanced at him. "You know—from people. And Ronan can leave, can try to find other pods and quieter waters, maybe in Ireland. He always said it wasn't safe here."

"He's right." It wasn't just Professor Foster. Every human was dangerous to Mara and her pod. Even Noah, with what he knew, could hurt them beyond saving. "If he finds a place for you, for the younglings, you should go."

Mara leaned harder against him. "That won't be for years. Ronan won't leave the younglings until they're old enough to protect themselves." She lowered her voice. "I'll be here next summer, when you come back. I'll wait for you."

All at once, he felt able to breathe again. "I'll wait too," he said.

He watched the waves crash beneath them, leaving dark pools among the rocks. Before this summer, he'd seen the land and the ocean as so different. He'd loved the ocean for how *other* it was. Here, though, everything mingled— water and rock, land and sea.

Mara tucked her foot under his, linking their dangling legs together. "It's like Gemm's stories," she said. "This can be our inbetween."

"Gemm says nobody stays in the inbetween forever."

"No. Not forever. But for now . . . what else can we do?"

They sat together in silence, listening to the steady drum of the waves on the cliffs.

Noah wondered when he'd come to hate the sound of his own breathing so much.

"I think we'll be fine," Mara said. "I've always wanted to be the Elder. I still want it. And I know there are things you want too, that you couldn't have if you stayed here." She pulled away to look at him. She ran a hand along his jaw line and kissed him lightly in the trail of her fingers.

Noah breathed in the scent of her hair, so much like the ocean. One day was so little time together.

He thought of Gemm and Maebh, of all the years they'd been apart, and his resolve strengthened. A school year was nothing compared to Gemm's forty years of absence — she'd married someone else, even, and they'd still found a way to be together in the end.

Noah kissed Mara again, her soft and salt-sprayed lips against his, and he tried to tell himself the kiss wasn't their last.

"Hey, big brother." Lo sidled up beside him at the railing.

Noah nodded slightly, keeping his gaze on the white foam breaking fifteen feet beneath him. The ferry's engine rumbled up through his bones, shaking his middle and vibrating in his neck and the top of his skull. He stared at the waves, at the almost-solid way they cracked against the sides of the boat. He refused to look back at the islands.

"Hey," Lo said again. "I get this — I mean, I do, but you're gonna freak Mom out if you're this angsty all week. You know the only way she'll stay sane when you're at college is if she thinks you're happy to go."

Noah glanced up, and the motion twisted his stomach. "Yeah, I know," he said, then swallowed the thickness in his throat. He'd never felt seasick before today.

"I mean, you're lucky she isn't making you live at home. When she heard about the knife, I seriously thought she was going to switch her apron strings for handcuffs."

Noah managed another brief nod.

"Okay." Lo frowned. "Shutting up now."

The waves crashed, one two, and the hull cut through them, one two. The rhythm was good, heartbeat-constant, and Noah thought if he could just fill his mind with it, he might distract himself from the links unraveling within him. Whatever Gemm had told him, he was sure his tie to Mara would be broken by the mainland. Maybe if he could stop thinking about it, though, he could hold on a little longer. One two, one two.

The waves curved into pale shoulders, breasts, lips, and the sound of their breaking was Mara's breath in his ear.

He winced. Though he was sure he'd be sick, he tore himself from the waves and looked up.

He could see the Shoals clearly behind him, the sun burning and glinting against the whitewashed buildings. They were small now, the hotel and the Center near-identical dots, the lighthouse a white splinter, and he could hardly make out Gemm's cottage at all. The waves blended into one another in the distance, so that Gosport Harbor looked smooth as sealskin.

He could feel Lo's worried gaze on him, and he turned away, facing west. The morning sun grew hot on the back of his head. The mainland drew its line on the horizon. Once they reached Portsmouth Harbor, that line would swallow him, and it would be the sea that was small in the distance, when he could see it at all. But for now it was only a line, warmed from the east by the sun, and Noah could not help but lean toward it, waiting to see what it would bring.